"I'm glad I could hel

"Call me Jake. Everyone

"Oh...um, okay." Elia bit her at him, looking unsure of what else to say. When her teeth released their hold, that part of her mouth was rosy and he was having a hard time not staring at it. At how moist and lush it looked, and how kissable—

Hell! This was why he hadn't wanted to see her right away. For some reason he was having trouble maintaining focus when she was around. He hadn't had that happen in a long time. Not since his ex.

He'd been fascinated by her looks too. But in the end, there hadn't been much underneath that pretty face, and disconnecting from her had brought only relief. He had a feeling with Elia he might discover there was more to her than met the eye.

Judging from that container on the counter there was. And he honestly didn't want to find out what lurked below the surface. Because if he thought it was hard not to notice things about her now, what would it be like in a month? Two months?

Dear Reader,

I think most of us have scars. Some of those scars are visible and some of them are deep inside, where they can't be seen. This sparked the idea for *Tempting the Off-Limits Nurse*.

Elia Pessoa has scars from a burn she received as a child. But she has other scars that no one can see. Scars that keep her from having long-term relationships. But along comes Dr. Jakob Callin, and as they treat badly injured patients in the hospital's burn unit, Jake coaxes her to reveal her secrets. All of them.

Thank you for joining Jake and Elia as they navigate the insecurities that come with relationships. As they learn that being vulnerable isn't always a bad thing. And maybe, just maybe, they will find something even more special along the way.

I hope you love their story as much as I loved writing about this special couple.

Love,

Tina Beckett

Tempting the
Off-Limits Nurse

―――――

TINA BECKETT

HARLEQUIN

MEDICAL
ROMANCE

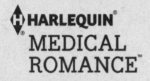

HARLEQUIN®
MEDICAL
ROMANCE™

Recycling programs
for this product may
not exist in your area.

ISBN-13: 978-1-335-59542-3

Tempting the Off-Limits Nurse

Copyright © 2024 by Tina Beckett

Harlequin Enterprises ULC
22 Adelaide St. West, 41st Floor
Toronto, Ontario M5H 4E3, Canada
www.Harlequin.com

Printed in U.S.A.

Three-time Golden Heart® Award finalist **Tina Beckett** learned to pack her suitcases almost before she learned to read. Born to a military family, she has lived in the United States, Puerto Rico, Portugal and Brazil. In addition to traveling, Tina loves to cuddle with her pug, Alex; spend time with her family; and hit the trails on her horse. Learn more about Tina from her website or friend her on Facebook.

Books by Tina Beckett

Harlequin Medical Romance

California Nurses

The Nurse's One-Night Baby

Starting Over with the Single Dad
Their Reunion to Remember
One Night with the Sicilian Surgeon
From Wedding Guest to Bride?
A Family Made in Paradise
The Vet, the Pup and the Paramedic
The Surgeon She Could Never Forget
Resisting the Brooding Heart Surgeon
A Daddy for the Midwife's Twins?

Visit the Author Profile page
at Harlequin.com for more titles.

To my family

PROLOGUE

SHE SHUFFLED BACKWARD, trying to coax her baby brother, who was almost ready to start walking, to come to her. All eyes were on whether or not he would succeed.

He burbled in laughter as one foot went forward, and he tottered for a second but remained on his feet.

"Keep going, Elia! He's doing it."

Buoyed by her mom's words, she took two more steps back, then three, as her brother continued to lurch toward her, big pauses between each step. She motioned to him. *"Venha aqui, Tomás!"*

He took another step. *Yes!*

Something caught at her foot, and she found herself staggering backward. She tried to catch herself but failed. She fell, still laughing in glee at her brother's accomplishment and that she was the one who'd succeeded in helping him where others had failed: to take his first steps.

She landed with a jolt that knocked the wind from her. An instant went by, and what had been shrieks of joy morphed into screams of agony as pain seared up one of her legs and her back.

Hands snatched her up and away from the heat, but the horrible stinging sensation continued and a weird scent filled the air. Vaguely she could hear her mother yelling for her father as she rocked Elia back and forth in her arms.

Her mind was numb, but she felt more hands grab her, hauling her away from her mom and racing away with her. A few seconds later, she was plunged into the icy stream behind their house and the burning stopped. She shut her eyes for a second in relief, only to open them and meet the gaze of her father. But there was no smile on his face. No words of encouragement. Only worry. And something else. Something worse.

It was at that second that her gaze went back to where she'd been helping her brother learn to walk and noticed the small bonfire they'd made to celebrate his first birthday was being put out by her *tio* and several other of her relatives with buckets of water from the stream. Her mother still sat on the log staring over at them in horror. It was then that Elia realized what had happened, just as her dad lifted her from the cooling water. She'd fallen into the firepit.

The burning began all over again, taking her thoughts captive as it engulfed her right leg and lower back. She moaned, clutching her dad's shirt before crying in earnest as the scorching sensation grew and grew and grew until nothing else existed.

She heard the word *hospital*, and then her dad was running with her in his arms, faster than she'd ever seen him run. Someone else drove their car as he held her in his arms the whole trip, his soothing words containing a shaky note that she'd never heard before.

He was big and strong. Stronger than anyone she knew. But now as he hunched over her, her *papá* just seemed…afraid.

CHAPTER ONE

JAKOB CALLIN LEANED over the bed of his patient, a teenager who'd been involved in an accident involving fireworks, and tried to decipher what the boy was saying. The reconstruction process on his jaw would be a long and arduous one. And the burns on his face would require some painful debriding and, very likely, skin grafting. The meds had eased some of the pain, but that combined with shock meant that he was trying to talk when he should be lying quiet. But he would have plenty of quiet days when his lower jaw was immobilized after surgery, leaving him to speak between clenched teeth.

"I want go rom…"

"Your room? You're already in your room."

The boy's eyes shut, and he shook his head, his right hand going up to his face. "Rom…" he tried again. "Go rom."

Jake took the boy's hand and pressed it back

onto the mattress, trying his damnedest to work out what he was getting so upset about. Maybe about his looks?

"We'll do all we can to make sure that your face is restored—"

"He's not worried about his face right now. He's worried about not getting to go to prom next week with his girlfriend, who is right outside this room."

The soft female voice came from over his shoulder, making him glance back. The slight accent caught him off guard, even more than her irritation, which was thinly veiled. Very thinly veiled, judging from the way her brows were pulled together in a sharp V.

He looked back at his patient who was now nodding his head.

So that's what he was trying to say. How had she…?

And what was she so irritated about?

Although he should be used to that by now. His ex's growing frustration every time he'd said "let's give it some time" when she'd wanted to start a family had soon sounded the death knell to their relationship. Frustration had soon given way to manipulation and then anger.

"Right now, you need to concentrate on

healing, Matt, okay? Do you want me to go out and talk to your girlfriend?" He hesitated. "What is her name?"

"Gracie. Her name is Gracie," came the voice from behind him. Again.

This time he didn't look. But surprisingly, and despite the impatience he'd seen in her expression, her face was already imprinted on his brain. With hair the color of his daddy's mahogany cigar box—the one Jake kept on his desk as a remembrance—the swirls and curves of those shiny locks had led his gaze straight to her face. Which was…beautiful. Even when she was angry. Or maybe *because* she was angry.

He kept his eyes on his patient. "Do you want me to talk to Gracie? Or maybe you'd like to see her for a few seconds."

This time the kid shook his head with a vehemence that told Jake everything he needed to know. He'd seen that look before on any number of his patients who didn't want their loved ones to see them like they were. Most didn't even want to look at themselves in the mirror in the beginning. Jake always did his best to change that.

"Okay. I get it. I'm sure she'll understand,

though. Do you want me to talk to her?" he asked again.

The boy gave a hard nod, but his eyes stared at the ceiling, not coming back to meet his.

Matt wasn't sure the girlfriend would understand. Jake wasn't sure, either. But hell. He hoped she would.

He swiveled on his stool to face the nurse who'd, in effect, scolded him. He was right about what she looked like. With delicate brows and cheekbones that seemed a mile high, she was a plastic surgeon's idea of perfection. Only Jake didn't deal in perfection. Not anymore. He simply did everything in his power to help his patients get back to living their lives in a way that caused them as little physical or emotional distress as possible.

Since this woman seemed to have definite ideas about what he should do, he arched a brow at her and inclined his head toward the other side of the room. He got up from his stool and moved to the area he'd indicated, halfway surprised when he turned and saw that she'd followed him.

"So do you want to go out and talk to Gracie, or do you think I'm capable of that, at least?"

Color rushed into her face, and he realized he'd embarrassed her. It wasn't his intent. He'd been trying to make a joke at his own expense. But then again, he didn't have much luck with that, either, when it came to talking to women, it seemed. At least not judging from the way his ex-girlfriend—a model—had chosen to break things off, moving out of their apartment when he'd been away at a conference. Looking back, he could see how poor of a match he and Samantha had been. He'd finally realized he'd been taken in by a pretty face—someone more interested in the status symbol of dating a doctor and what that could give her than she'd been in him as a person. He was pretty sure the having children angle had been her way of manipulating him into staying when it looked like their relationship was beginning to fracture. She'd obviously never expected him to say no to the request.

Whatever the reasons, he never wanted to go through a messy breakup like that again.

"I'm sorry if I…" The nurse's words trailed away, that same slight accent coming through that had caught his attention before. He was around people of all nationalities so he should be used to accents. But this one was a little different from what he was accustomed to, he just wasn't sure how.

"No. I'm sorry. We seem to have gotten off

on the wrong foot. You're new here at the hospital?"

She hesitated. "Sort of. I've been here for two weeks, but in the scheme of things, you could say I'm new. To the hospital, anyway, although I've lived in Texas ever since I was his age." She indicated their patient on the bed.

"Sorry not to have welcomed you to Westlake Memorial before now, then. Have you been in this department the whole two weeks?"

If so, he wasn't sure how their paths had not crossed yet.

"Yes. We've worked together on a couple of other patients."

Hell, he was slipping. He normally prided himself on noticing the little things and chatting with the nurses he worked with. But evidently not this time. "In that case, I'm sorry again." He glanced at the badge hanging from her lanyard. "Eliana Pessoa?"

She corrected the pronunciation of her last name, although this time she smiled. And those high cheekbones carved out hollows beneath them that made his mouth go dry.

Get it together, Callin.

"So what do you suggest we tell Gracie?"

"The truth. But I wouldn't make any promises you can't keep about his appearance."

"I don't do that, since every patient's body reacts differently to surgery."

There was a pause. "Yes, it does."

Something about the way she said that made him glance at her a little closer. Maybe a little too close, since she looked behind her before taking a step back. "Well, I need to check on a couple of other patients. Are you sure you don't want me to talk to Gracie?"

"I've been doing this a while and haven't had too many complaints, so I think I can do it." He smiled to soften the words.

"Okay, then. I'll see you later."

With that, she walked toward the door, a hitch in her step that was as faint as her accent, and something that he probably wouldn't have caught if he hadn't been staring at her.

Before she walked out, she looked at the patient. "I'll check on you in a bit, Matt. Try to get some rest."

The boy somehow managed to give her a thumbs-up sign, which made her smile again before she swept out of the room.

What had just happened here?

He wasn't sure, but it seemed he'd just met a nurse who advocated for her patients as strongly as he prided himself on doing. Not that Westlake wasn't full of nurses who did everything possible to help the patients under their care. There was just an empathy…an understanding to her manner that caught his attention.

Or was it her looks?

Was he really that shallow? Hell, he hoped not, although Samantha had caught his attention for the exact same reason. And he didn't like it.

So he was going to do his best to tread lightly around Eliana Pessoa. Because another thing Jake prided himself on was learning from his mistakes. No matter how painful that process might be.

Elia was glad to be out of there. She wasn't sure why, but being around Dr. Callin made her jittery in a way that made her grumpy. She was pretty sure some of that had come through when she'd addressed him, but it was either that or let him get under her skin, where she wasn't sure she could shake him off.

The fact that he couldn't even remember working with her those other times shouldn't make her feel invisible. There were enough nurses coming in and out of rooms that it was probably hard to keep them all straight. And from what she understood, he was a plastic surgeon who had shifted over to specializing in burns and reconstruction from traumatic injuries. Like Matt's, though the teen's burns were almost as significant as his shattered jaw. That was one thing she hadn't had to deal with as a child when she was in a burn unit in her home country of Portugal and undergoing surgery after surgery. Despite all of that effort, her right leg looked and behaved quite a bit differently from her left one. But at least it was still there. Things could have been so much worse.

She lowered herself into a chair in the hospital's Mocha Café and took her first sip of coffee. Hot and sweet, the espresso didn't have quite the bite the ones that her mom made for her at home had, but it was still good. Or maybe she'd just become Americanized.

Stretching her leg out in front of her, she tried to relieve a little of the neuralgia that being on her feet all day caused while, at the same time, keeping a slight bend in her knee so as not to aggravate the contracture that the scarring from her burns had caused. She couldn't straighten it all the way, and her last doctor had told her that after all this time, things were pretty much set in stone unless they went in and did some cutting and regrafting. There was no guarantee that it would help, since her body didn't deal kindly with scar tissue—a result of genetics.

She took another sip of her coffee, relishing the heat that washed down her throat and hit her stomach. Resting her chin on the palm of her free hand, she took another sip, letting her eyes close.

She was bone tired. She still had two hours left of her shift, but her nursing supervisor had taken one look at her as she came out of Matt's room and had told her to take a break. Elia hadn't argued. She hadn't wanted to watch Dr. Callin go over to talk to Matt's girlfriend.

Maybe she shouldn't have specialized in burns in nursing school. But it was where she felt like she could do the most good. She'd gone through some of what her patients were experiencing, although maybe not to the degree that Matt would, since the reminders of her injuries were hidden from view. So many of their patients didn't have that luxury. Some were even fighting for their lives.

She sensed more than felt someone's presence and opened her eyes to find Jakob Callin had entered the room and glanced her way.

Deus! Just what she needed…for him to find her practically asleep. Although she hadn't been really. For Elia, "resting her eyes" wasn't a euphemism for sleeping. It really did help to shut out the world for a few moments and quiet her soul.

He changed his trajectory and headed toward her. She braced herself, bending her right knee until her legs were together under the table. She didn't know why she was wary of him noticing something like that, but she was. When she was dressed she could pretend she wasn't different. And she wasn't, in so many ways, but even after all these years she still got self-conscious about it, which was why she rarely ever wore a swimsuit or shorts, even in the middle of a Dallas summer, when the heat could take your breath away.

When she'd arrived in the States, there had already been so much different about her besides her leg: her grasp of English, being the new kid in a school where friendships were already formed, wearing yoga pants instead of gym shorts to PE classes. So there was a tiny part of her that felt that people were looking for any sign of weakness, even if they weren't. It made her strive to excel in everything she did, including her job.

Dr. Callin arrived at her table and glanced down at her. "Just wanted to say I'm sorry for not properly welcoming you to the team.

Sheryll confirmed you've been here for two weeks already. That's not like me."

Had he not believed her?

"It's okay. Really." Another thing Elia tended to do was stay in the background where she was less likely to be noticed. So it was pretty unlike her to go up and challenge someone who was in authority over her. But Matt's case had touched her heart, for some reason. Maybe because she was willing his girlfriend to stick it out with him. To not care that he might look a little different—once all of the surgeries were over and done with—from the guy she'd first been attracted to.

While Elia had never actually had a man drop her once they found out about her scarring, she had caught them avoiding touching those areas, probably in deference to her feelings. And one of the men she'd dated had actually kept the covers pulled up over their legs whenever they'd made love. All it did was make her even more self-conscious. She'd stopped seeing him soon afterward.

Well, it didn't matter, because she wasn't dating Dr. Callin.

"It's not okay. Do you have time for me to join you for a few minutes? Sheryll said she's already given you the rundown on the department, but I'd like to get your thoughts on a few things."

So maybe she was going to be lambasted for challenging him in public. Although she didn't really see it that way. She'd merely been helping him understand what the patient was saying. The way she'd wished people had been able to understand her when she'd first arrived at her new home in Austin. Matt was going to have to learn to talk all over again once his jaw was reconstructed, especially if his tongue had been affected by the explosion.

"Um…sure." If she said no, he was going to wonder why. And she was going to have to work with him. No matter that he made her insides tuck and roll for some reason.

With thick hair—already peppered with some gray—that was swept up and over his forehead, bright blue eyes and some scruff on his jaw, the man was an imposing figure. He looked strong and sure and in control. And for someone like Elia, who in her twenty-six years had gone through life events where she felt completely out of control, he was intimidating, even though he probably didn't mean to be.

"Great. I'll be right back. Do you want anything while I'm up getting my coffee?"

"No, I'm good, but thank you."

When her dad, who was an engineer, had been approached to work for a company in the States, he'd traveled back and forth from Portugal to Austin for close to a year before her mom had said enough was enough and that if he liked his job that much, they would relocate so they could all be together. And so began the second big upheaval in her life. First her leg. Then leaving behind her friends and everything she knew.

But she didn't regret the move. She missed her relatives in Castelo Branco, but she went back to visit her home country every couple of years, usually jigging her holiday time so it coincided with her parents' when they flew to Portugal.

She watched Dr. Callin as he walked and ordered coffee, which was handed to him in a big American-sized mug rather than the much smaller demitasse her own espresso had come in. She drained the rest of it, grimacing when the now lukewarm liquid hit her tongue.

When she'd decided she wanted to work in a hospital with a burn unit, the huge hospital in Dallas was the obvious choice. Her mom had been afraid her career would make her relive the trauma of being burned over and over, but surprisingly it didn't. It made her feel stronger, if anything, like she was turning something terrible into something useful by helping people who found themselves in a position like the one she'd been in throughout her childhood. And strangely, it sometimes helped when people found out she really did know what it felt like to undergo some of those not-so-fun procedures.

He was headed back to her table, so she took a deep breath and braced herself for a barrage of questions about why she'd chosen the field, etc.

He slid into the chair across from her, and the click of his cup as he set it down on the table seemed extraordinarily loud, even though it hadn't been. And the silence that followed seemed horribly, terribly empty. She racked her brain to think of something to say.

"So how long have you been at Westlake?"

His cup stopped midway to his lips as if surprised by her question. "I've been here ever since I started med school."

Of course, that made sense. Westlake Memorial was a big teaching hospital. She'd actually been surprised to be hired on by them, since they probably could handpick their staff just from the students who came through their doors. But she'd been top of her class, too, even though the school she'd gone to wasn't quite as prestigious as the one attached to Westlake.

He took a sip of his own coffee. "And Sheryll tells me you're originally from Austin?"

That made her smile. She knew she still had an accent so there was no way that he thought she was born and raised in Austin. "Not originally, no. I was born in Portugal, but my dad got a job in Austin, so we moved to the States when I was just starting high school."

"And you didn't want to go back after you graduated?"

The question surprised her. "My closest family members are here, although I go back to Portugal to visit when I can."

He nodded and didn't say anything for a minute. Suddenly she regretted slugging back the rest of her coffee. At least it would have given her something to do with her hands. She wished he would just get to the point of whatever he wanted to say to her. Did he drink coffee with every new staff member?

"We normally have cake for new staff members." He smiled as if reading her thoughts. "Maybe that's what threw me and why I didn't realize you had just come here. But Sheryll said you asked her not to do anything special."

In reality, Elia hated being in the spotlight.

Her family already knew not to signal waiters when it was her birthday. The thought of a group of strangers gathering around her table and singing "Happy Birthday" to her wasn't her idea of fun, although Tomás loved it. Her mom had once told her that she'd wanted a big family with lots of children, but that it hadn't been in the cards, since she'd ended up having a hysterectomy in her early thirties due to endometrial cancer. It had been caught early, though, and her mom had been cancer free ever since, thank God.

She shrugged. "I figured I could get to know people on my own terms." Feeling she needed to add something more, she said, "I'm really happy to be at Westlake."

"And we're happy you're here." His smile grew. "And you really saved my bacon when you helped me understand what our patient was saying."

Okay, so by context she understood what he meant by saving his bacon, but she'd always thought it funny how different languages had expressions that made little or no sense. Like *falar pelos cotovelos* in Portuguese. It meant to talk too much, but translated literally it meant your elbows were doing the talking.

"I remember what it felt like not to be understood. But I'm truly sorry if I spoke up where I shouldn't have." She was doing her best not to notice how his smile softened the hard lines of his face. How it was the tiniest bit crooked, the right side tilting slightly higher than the left, or how it made little crinkles radiate out from the corners of his eyes. It was damned attractive.

"No, you should have. I like to think our unit is a team. We help each other out as needed. So if you ever think I'm not seeing a situation like I should, please bring it to my attention."

"Okay, thank you. Anything else I should know about the burn unit?"

"I want input. If you've heard about a new treatment that has some pretty solid studies behind it…that you think we should try on a more difficult case, feel free to speak up. We all have our own little groups where we talk about work and interesting articles or information gets passed around. I want our team to stay cutting-edge. To excel, for the benefit of our patients."

So he wasn't just looking to be on top. She could respect that. In fact, she did respect it as long as they didn't just turn out to be empty words. Time would tell. But she really did hope he was telling the truth.

"I will." And she would. Even though she

didn't like being in the spotlight, she did want what was best for her patients, so if she thought another technique would work better, she wouldn't hesitate to say so. Well…she might hesitate, but she would speak up.

But what she wouldn't do was get too attached to that smile or do her best to make it reappear whenever she was around him. Because to do that was to head down a dangerous path. And she'd already seen where those roads led time and time again. They led to heartache and the fear of loss.

No, Jakob Callin's smile was best saved for those who would appreciate it for what it was. The simple movement of muscles over a scaffold of bone. It might transform his face, but in the scheme of things it meant very little. And she would do well to remember that.

CHAPTER TWO

POSTERS WERE PLASTERED all over the hospital. The annual biking event to raise money for the hospital's different departments was happening in just a couple of weeks. Jake sighed. The announcements had been up for a while, but he'd kind of looked past them until he'd received a memo in his mailbox reminding him to talk the event up in his own department. He was sure every other department chair had received the same notice.

This in combination with the influx of new students they would get in the spring and fall did great things for the hospital, but it increased his workload, sometimes to the breaking point.

It wasn't that he didn't like to ride bicycles. In fact, it was his exercise of choice. He went out at least a couple of times a week to relieve built-up stress. He'd just put new tires on his bike actually, and not for the biking event. Just because the treads had grown thin from use. And once a week he chose to ride his bike the ten miles to work and back. It helped get his blood pumping and got his mind ready for the day at hand. And on the trek back home, he rode at a leisurely pace where he paid attention to the world around him, the way he couldn't do when driving his SUV.

Maybe Sheryll would have some new ideas on how to encourage people to get involved. They normally hung a sign-up sheet behind the nurse's station for staff, but they were encouraged to let the patients know it was open to anyone who wanted to attend. Families with kids often made it an outing for all ages. It wasn't unusual to see a bike towing a baby trailer.

There was nothing cutthroat about the event. Yes, the first one to cross the finish line did get their picture put up at the hospital and usually got a write-up in the local paper. But presenting it as a day of fun to the families of patients who were terribly injured was tricky business, and he didn't want to come across as glib or uncaring. Or that all he cared about was the hospital's PR machine. Because his patients were more important to him than any fundraiser. If it were up to him, he would just let the hospital posters speak for themselves, but he understood where the administration was coming from. It was their job to raise the money for some of their pet projects and plan it around times when there were big repairs needed at the hospital.

He got off the elevator at the fourth floor and headed for the desk. Only Sheryll was nowhere in sight. Nor was anyone else. He frowned at the eerie quiet until he glanced at his watch and saw that it was time to dispense meds for those patients who needed them. Then he spotted a huge glass container with a matching lid perched on the desk of the nurse's station. It looked like an oversize apothecary jar. But unlike the ones that held cotton balls or tongue depressors that were set up in the patients' rooms, these held cookies. Cookies with a layer of smooth blue frosting on top and...bikes. Bikes of all different colors, one per cookie. He frowned, looking closer. Not only were there bicycles on the sweet treats, but there were also clouds and some of them contained tiny flowers along a bike path. On a plate next to the jar was a pair of tongs, evidently to use when fishing out the cookies. In front of the jar a note was propped up saying

Help Yourself. On the other side of the jar were flyers about the bike festival.

Sheryll came out of one of the patient's rooms and spotted him. "So you found them, did you? I heard through the grapevine yesterday that those wonderful notices were going out yesterday, and we thought we'd get a little jump on things, so you wouldn't have to give your yearly pep talk. I know how much you like those."

He smiled. "Probably as much as the staff like hearing them."

He wasn't sure what he would do without the department's head nurse. She was dedicated to both the patients and their nurses, going to bat for both whenever the need arose. It was why the burn unit had such a small turnover of employees.

But the cookies...

"Did you make these?" he asked.

"Me? Of course not. I like to cook, but not bake, much to my husband's chagrin."

He tilted his head and glanced at the jar again. They did look professionally made. They even had lettering at the top that said Bike Festival along with the date. But if she'd only heard about the notices yesterday, there wouldn't have been enough time to order these, would there? "Then who?"

"It was Elia. I gathered the nurses around yesterday and asked for ideas. She offered to bake cookies. But I never thought they'd be this fancy. Or this good. Try one."

He took the tongs and pulled a cookie out, glancing at it. With a red bike that sported a basket on the front of it, he was again struck by the detail. These must have taken hours to make. Then he took a bite and his eyes widened.

This wasn't your normal sugar cookie. It was lemony. And light. And so good.

"Was I right?"

"Unfortunately, yes. Because they're really too fancy to eat."

"That hasn't stopped anyone who's come by the desk. We've refilled the jar once already."

He turned to look at her. "You mean she made more than just these?"

"Yes, and she promised to keep them in good supply over the next couple of weeks."

"She didn't mention anything about doing this when I had coffee with her yesterday."

Sheryll's eyes widened. "You took her out for coffee?"

His brain shifted into high gear at her tone.

"No, I happened to see her in the hospital's café, and we chatted for a few minutes. About work," he added in case she might think there was anything more behind it.

"Whew. Good to know. I was starting to think you were developing a soft spot under that tough exterior."

No, he wasn't. At least he hoped not. That was the last thing he wanted. Especially where the newest member of his team was concerned. He'd already noticed far too much about her.

"I think you know me better than that."

She laughed. "I know a couple of women in other departments say that you're a tough nut to crack. Not that they wouldn't mind trying."

"Not happening. Even if I were interested in dating—which I'm not—I wouldn't date anyone at the hospital. Too messy." He wasn't sure anything could be messier than his relationship with Samantha, though. That had been a fiasco and a PR nightmare.

A woman with a child walked by and spotted the cookies and smiled at them. "This is so nice, thank you."

Sheryll smiled. "They're as good as they look. Help yourselves."

The mom took two cookies and napkins to go with them, and then she picked up a flyer.

Once she left, the nurse turned to him. "Better than having to verbally promote it, yes?"

"Yes. Please tell Elia thank you for me."

"You can do that yourself. She's headed this way."

He wasn't sure if Sheryll noticed the way his eyes shut for a second as he gave an inward groan. He'd been hoping not to run into her first thing, and he wasn't sure why. But maybe it was better just to do it now and get it over with.

Turning, he saw she indeed was headed this way with one of the digital devices they used to record patient information on.

Was it his imagination or was her face pink? He realized he was still holding half of the cookie he'd gotten out a few minutes ago. Surely she wasn't embarrassed about them.

"I was just telling Sheryll that I appreciate you providing these. They're delicious. You made them and decorated them all last night?"

She gave a quick shrug. "Portugal is famous for their pastries and bread. My mom actually drove up from Austin and helped since she still loves to bake from scratch. She was a pastry chef when we lived in Europe. You wouldn't believe the bread oven my dad imported from

Portugal for her for their twenty-fifth anni-
versary. It's better than anything you'll find
here in the States. I'll have to bring you some
sometime."

He paused as he tried to think of what to say.
But he must have hesitated too long because
she jumped in with, "For everyone here on the
floor, I mean."

If anything, the color in her cheeks deep-
ened. He hadn't meant to imply that her words
held any hidden message. "I'm looking forward to trying it. But the cookies are a perfect advertisement for the bike festival. Thank
you again."

She smiled. "It was fun. I'm so busy that I
don't often have time to spend doing something like that with Mom. So it's a great opportunity."

Sheryll propped her elbows on the upper
portion of the desk. "Jake hates having to promote hospital doings. Things like this take a
lot of pressure off him."

"Yes, it does," he murmured.

"I'm glad I could help, Dr. Callin."

Had she been using his title ever since she
started working at the hospital?

"Call me Jake. Everyone does."

"Oh...um, okay." Elia bit her lip and glanced

at him, looking unsure of what else to say. When her teeth released its hold, that part of her mouth was rosy and he was having a hard time not staring at it. At how moist and lush it looked, and how kissable—

Hell! This was why he hadn't wanted to see her right away. For some reason he was having trouble maintaining focus when she was around. He hadn't had that happen in a long time. Not since his ex. He'd been fascinated by her looks, too. But in the end, there hadn't been much underneath that pretty face, and disconnecting from her had brought only relief. He had a feeling with Elia he might discover there was more to her than met the eye.

Judging from that container on the counter there was. And he honestly didn't want to find out what lurked below the surface. Because if he thought it was hard not to notice things about her now, what would it be like in a month? Two months?

Maybe it would all blow over and he'd simply get used to having her around. Get used to seeing her like any other staff member here at Westlake Memorial.

At least he could hope that was the case. He turned away and took the last bite of his cookie and shook his head. For some reason he had his doubts that it would be that easy.

Or that quick.

Watching Jake bite into that cookie had sent goose bumps over her in a way that she wasn't used to. And she didn't like it. She really had just wanted to help. But now she wasn't so sure that had been a good idea. Yes, she and her mom had had a blast making the cookies. But when he'd looked uncomfortable at her offer of bringing him some of her mother's bread, she'd been mortified. Had he thought she'd been hitting on him or something?

God. Every time she saw him now, she was going to wonder if he was thinking about that nurse who'd been desperately seeking his attention in any way that she could get it.

You're overthinking things, Elia.

She knew she was, but it was probably because she'd noticed him more than she should have.

And making the cookies had had nothing to do with him and everything to do with her patients. She also planned to support the event by participating in it. The movements on a bicycle were more comfortable for her than most exercises, since her right leg didn't have to straighten completely, unlike running or power walking. Swimming ran a close second, since the water helped support her injured leg.

Sheryll patted her on the shoulder. "He can be kind of gruff, but he means well."

So maybe she hadn't been overthinking things after all, if the head nurse had noticed something.

"I just hope he didn't think I was being overly friendly."

This time the other woman tilted her head. "Overly friendly?"

"By saying I would bring in some bread that my mom makes."

"No, I don't think that was it. I think he just doesn't know how to say thank you very well."

They moved away from the desk.

A call button went off. "That's Matt's room," Sheryll said.

They both stopped midstride as Matt's mom poked her head out of his room and said, "Please! We need help!"

She and Sheryll rushed over and Veronica moved to let them inside. "He just started shaking and can't stop."

Sure enough, the teen was visibly shuddering, his face red, eyes huge with fear. Elia was the first to the bed and as soon as she touched him realized why. "He's burning up. Can you page Dr. Callin?"

"Yep."

Matt was lucid, although clearly feeling the effects of a fever. And when she got his temp, she saw she was right. He was at 103.6. The biggest fear, besides tissue trauma from an injury like his, was infection. And although they hadn't seen signs of any so far, with burns it wasn't always easy to judge. The burn damage itself caused redness and inflammation that were also markers for infectious processes. And burns caused exudate that could act as a petri dish, the moist environment ideal for growing various microbes.

The teen wanted blankets, but that was the opposite of what he needed, so she stripped off his covers, despite his protests.

"I know it's uncomfortable, Matt, but we need to get you cooled down." It had been almost an hour since she'd given him his meds, and his temperature then had been near normal.

Just as she was getting some cool moist cloths to put on his forehead and wrists, Jake swept into the room. Evidently Sheryll had already briefed him, because he got right to the point. "What's his reading?"

"One hundred and three point six, as of five minutes ago."

"Let's take it again."

She quickly repeated the process and frowned. "One hundred and three point nine…"

"Chart?"

Elia handed over the digital device and Jake perused it for a second. "Let's pull the cephalosporin and see if that brings it down. When's he due for his next dose?"

Although a couple of the medications Matt was on could induce a fever under certain conditions, it was a fairly common side effect with cephalosporin. She could see why Jake wanted to start by changing that up rather than assume that infection was setting in.

"He got his last dose of that one at midnight, so we're looking at noon today."

She'd noticed that Jake didn't wear a traditional lab coat but opted for street clothes instead. And today he was wearing a burgundy polo shirt and black jeans. With his swept-back hair, the combination was stunning and she had to force herself to remain on task.

He glanced at her. "Okay, good. If that's the cause, the fever should start subsiding almost immediately as the meds clear his system. If that does it, we'll change over to another class of antibiotics."

She nodded. "Anything else you want me to do?"

"The rest of his vitals are good?"

"I was just going to check." Elia measured his blood pressure and other vitals, and although his pulse was a little higher than it had been earlier, that could be caused by shivering and fear. She relayed everything to Jake as she took them.

Matt's mom broke in. "Is he going to be okay?"

"I'm hoping his fever is just a side effect of his antibiotics. We're going to pull those and see if the fever comes down. If not, we'll reevaluate and make a few alterations to his medications. I want to be cautious, but I don't want to throw more antibiotics at it until we've settled on a 'why' for this spike in temp."

He turned back to their patient. "Can I look you over, Matt?"

The boy nodded, and Elia had to admire the way the plastic surgeon peeled back the moist bandages they'd been using over the wounds. He was scheduled for a debridement later this afternoon, and hopefully they could get started on some of the surgeries to repair his shattered jaw, which would be done by one of their orthopedic surgeons. Jake would follow up with the skin grafting.

Once he'd finished his exam, he swiveled the stool back to look at Veronica. "I don't see anything overly concerning at the moment, but I'll put in a call to Dr. Julle and ask him to come in and have a look, as well, okay?"

Elia hadn't yet met Dr. Julle, but then again there were quite a few staff members she didn't know yet. Even if she'd let them get a cake for her, it would have just been for the staff in the burn unit and whatever other doctors happened to wander through on that particular day, so there was no guarantee she would have met him even then.

She walked Jake to the door. "Do you want me to use cool compresses?"

"Yes. If it rises above one hundred and four page me again and we'll use more aggressive measures. We're nearing the twelve-hour mark, so we should start seeing a reversal soon if it's the cephalosporin."

"Okay."

Sheryll had already left the room to go see to other patients, leaving her alone with Jake. Their arms brushed as he reached for the door and Elia had to repress a shudder that was every bit as strong as Matt's had been.

Nossa Senhora! What was wrong with her today?

His voice when it came was low, his head close to her ear. "If you see anything unusual at all, I want you to call me. I hope this is a simple case of drug-induced fever, but if it's not, I want to get in there and figure this thing out. Who knows what was introduced into the wounds when the shrapnel from the exploded firework hit him."

"Are you thinking sepsis?"

He nodded for her to go out of the room with him. She did and let him close the door behind them. "Not yet. But I want to go ahead and draw some blood. His pulse rate is elevated, but that could just be from the fever itself, since his blood pressure is still in the normal range."

"Those were my thoughts, as well."

He smiled. "Were they?"

She might have thought he was poking fun at her, but there was no hint of arrogance in the words. Instead, it was like he appreciated having another voice added to his own. Her face heated. Some doctors didn't really want to hear from the nursing staff, they just wanted their orders carried out, but she sensed Jake wasn't like that. Maybe because of the way he'd been chatting with Sheryll. But it was more than that. It was the way Sheryll had gathered the staff to help ease some of the administrative burden off the plastic surgeon when it came to the bike festival. The head nurse respected Jake. Liked him, even. It was evident in how she spoke about him.

So she gave him a smile of her own. "Yes, but it's good to know that so far Matt is doing okay."

"Any word from his girlfriend?"

This time Elia bit her lip, a bad habit of hers whenever something was concerning. She quickly stopped when she saw Jake's eyes go there.

"No, but she's probably in school right now. Veronica told me they've been, er…" She had to think of the English term Veronica had used. "Sweet on each other since middle school, so I'm hoping she'll be supportive."

"Me, too. It will help in his recovery."

"Yes. It will." She could think of her teenage years when she'd had some revision surgery on her leg once they moved to the States. They were able to ease some of the contracture, but not all of it, due to her genetic makeup. She'd had one boyfriend in high school, but only one and he'd been uneasy about her burn scars, although she never wore shorts to school and for gym she wore track pants at the request of her parents to make things easier for her. So she'd still felt different back then, but the thought of wearing shorts and exposing the thing that made her feel the most vulnerable was unthinkable. And thankfully her parents had had a pool in their backyard so she could put on a swimsuit without being seen by anyone but her family.

That was another strike against her with her boyfriend—that she wouldn't swim with him when he came to the house, even though he said he didn't care about her scars. In reality, she didn't believe him. She hadn't believed anyone back then. They lasted about six months and then he broke things off with her.

Jake touching her hand not only jerked her out of her thoughts, it made her jerk her hand away.

He frowned. "Sorry. You just looked like you were a thousand miles away, and I was just going to ask you again to let me know if Matt's condition changes, in either direction."

"I will, and you don't have to be sorry. You were right. You just startled me." She didn't elaborate on what she'd been thinking about, and she certainly didn't want him to think she was that uptight about being casually touched. She wasn't. And what she'd said was true. It had just startled her. Nothing more.

Or was it? She'd had that same startled reaction when their arms had accidentally touched. Like electricity had shot through her system. In a good way.

Which meant it was the opposite of good. And she'd better get ahold of herself. If she jerked every time they came in contact with each other, he was bound to notice. And if she'd been worried about him thinking she was after him before, she'd be doubly nervous of that if she kept having some weird reaction to him.

And the last thing she wanted was to actually develop some kind of crush on the man.

She shook off the thoughts, before he noticed that she was spacing out again. "Well, I'd better get those compresses going. I'll keep you apprised of his condition."

"Appreciated. See you later."

And with that he turned and was gone before she could say anything else. But not before he cast a glance in the direction of her cookie jar. For some reason, that made her smile as she went back in the room to take care of her patient and to pray that Jake was right about the reason for the boy's fever.

CHAPTER THREE

JAKE COASTED ONTO the hospital grounds, using the designated bike path that continued from the road onto the medical center's property. Matt's fever from the other day, as suspected, had been the result of the cephalosporin, and yesterday, he'd had the first surgery on his lower jaw. The damaged teeth on the right side had had to be removed, which he knew the boy had been upset about, but with the advent of dental implants, no one would ever notice. The more worrisome thing was hoping the bone graft taken from the teen's fibula would take. It had been a multi-surgeon effort, with Dr. Julle performing the bone graft in consultation with a dental surgeon who would later do the tooth implants.

Jake had done the skin graft surgery to cover the site on the boy's leg, harvesting tissue from his buttock. Everything had gone according to plan. If all went well, he would have normal function to his jaw.

Heading toward the bike rack the hospital had installed in the grass near one of the main entrances, he saw that someone else had just stopped their bike and was hooking it up.

He slowed further as he came up behind her and called out to let her know he was there. She turned to look and Jake jerked on the handlebars and nearly toppled his bike. It was Elia. In her Lycra biker pants, tennis shoes and a racing top that bared her shoulders, she looked very different from the nurse who'd sported loose scrubs the other times he'd seen her. She was sexy as hell.

Not that she hadn't been that before, but she was even more stunning.

She smiled at him. "Careful. You might wind up in your own ER. The thing about never forgetting how to ride a bike is we're sometimes a little more wobbly when we get on after not having ridden for a while."

Not having ridden? Hell, he rode here once a week. "You just startled me, that's all."

Funny that those were the same words she'd used when she'd jerked away from him the other day.

"Okay."

She didn't believe him. Why did it matter? But for some reason it did. "I actually ride in to work fairly often."

But he was almost positive he'd never seen her bike here before. It was a sleek red racing-style bike with black handlebars and spokes, which showed that she knew a thing or two about bicycles.

"Ah, got it. I actually haven't tried that before today. But I thought with the festival coming up, riding in would give me a chance to train without having to make a special effort." She finished attaching her chain to the bike stand, then slung a backpack over her arm. "The only pain is having to change clothes when I get here."

And there it was. The flash of an image that he'd done his best to prevent. Of her slowly rolling those tight pants over her hips and down her legs. He gritted his teeth to banish it.

"Yep, I get it. I only live about ten miles out, so mornings are okay. But the afternoon heat definitely takes it out of you on the way back home." And he didn't say that he had an office with his own bathroom to change in because that sounded kind of privileged. And really, it was. It was on the tip of his tongue to offer to let her use his space, but he knew if he did, that image he'd just suppressed would come roaring back whenever he went into his office.

"Where's a good place to ride around here? I'm from Austin, so that's all I know as far as areas to ride."

"It depends on what you're looking for and how far you want to go. Several of the bike shops offer group rides, including one that I'm in that does a longer Saturday ride. It begins and ends at University Park and makes a big loop around the Dallas/Fort Worth Airport. You're welcome to come along if you want to."

He wasn't sure why he'd offered, but he did. And now that he had, he felt he needed to add some more details, just in case. "It's a forty-seven-mile trip."

"Not too bad. I've done longer, but they've normally been in the spring or late fall when it's a little cooler." She paused for a second. "Do you mind my coming along? I promise I'll find my own niche, but it would be nice to see a familiar face the first time."

Something about the hesitant way she said it made him glad he'd asked. "I don't mind at all. You'll find most of the biking community in Dallas to be pretty welcoming."

"So you do this a lot?"

"It's something I enjoy."

She nodded. "Me, too."

Her eyes searched his face for a long second before turning away. "Well, I'd better head in." Then she turned back. "I was off yesterday. How did Matt's jaw surgery go?"

He locked his own bike and they headed in together. "It went well. And the girlfriend came for it."

She still had that little hitch in her gait. He couldn't tell exactly where it was coming from but seemed to be in her right leg. It was barely noticeable, but it was there just the same. Even so, she had no problem keeping up with him.

"That is so great. Has he agreed to see her yet?"

He nodded. "Finally, when he came out of surgery. But he was pretty bandaged up so maybe he wasn't as worried about what she'd see." He'd seen that in many patients who'd undergone some type of life-altering event, such as a severe burn.

They got on the elevator and Jake pushed the button for the fourth floor. "Did you get to do any of the skin grafts yet?"

"Just the one to cover the donor site, where they harvested the bone. The facial reconstruction grafts will need to be done a little later."

They arrived on the floor and got off. "So you're on for Saturday?"

"I am. What time?"

"The ride starts at eight. Come with a water bottle and any snacks you might need."

She smiled, and those areas below her cheeks hollowed out again, showing off her beautiful bone structure. "Yep. I'll come prepared. Thanks again for the invitation."

"You're welcome. See you on the floor."

"See you."

As he passed the cookie jar, he noted that they were almost gone. She'd said she was off yesterday. But he also didn't want her to feel like she needed to keep supplying the floor with free snacks, especially since they took so much effort. He made a mental note to mention it when he saw her next. And he also put Saturday's ride in his calendar. There was no need to register, it was just a "show up" kind of thing. Sometimes there was a leader from the shop, sometimes it was self-guided. There were folks who did this every week and could kind of let newcomers in on what to expect and where the places were to wait for help, if needed. They also liked to know if you opted to quit early so they didn't worry about something having happened and send a rider out to try to find you. Just normal trip etiquette types of things.

But for now, he wanted to review patient charts and plan his day. He had two surgeries today that had nothing to do with burns. One was the repair of a cleft palate. And the other was a revision surgery for someone who'd had an earlier surgery for skin cancer at another hospital that had healed badly and left a larger scar than necessary. He felt with an hour's worth of work he could coax the skin to give a little more and to lie a little flatter across her cheek.

As he changed his own clothes, he wondered again about Elia's leg and if her limp had to do with muscle weakness. If so, was a long ride going to be taxing for her? She said she rode regularly, so he assumed she'd done this before. But maybe he should ask.

No. She was an adult who could make her own choices. If she felt she could do the ride, then who was he to second-guess that? He certainly wouldn't want to have it done for him.

He chuckled. Of course she'd thought he was just starting to ride a bike again. That's what he got for letting her get under his skin.

And she was doing it. No matter how much

he might try to deny it. Would Saturday make it even worse?

He could only hope not. Again, he wondered if being around her might be a good thing, almost like a desensitization process that made him notice her less.

It might work. But then again, he never really noticed when other women wore biking shorts and cool tops. But at least it wouldn't be a surprise on Saturday when she came.

And this next time, he'd keep hold of his composure and show her that he really did know his stuff when it came to cycling.

She arrived at Walter's Bike Shop on Saturday morning and parked her car. There were several people already here, but there was no sign of Jake, yet. Maybe he wasn't coming. No, he'd seen her again at work yesterday toward the end of the day and said he'd see her here. She'd almost backed out. But then she felt like she'd have to explain why she didn't want to go, and she really *didn't* have a good explanation other than he still made her uneasy. Every time she'd seen him over the last day or two, he'd still had the power to make her face heat up and her nipples tighten. That was the worst thing of all. She'd had to choose a specific sports bra today, one that did a good job keeping that kind of thing under wraps. It wasn't the most comfortable contraption to wear or the easiest to get into. But at least he wouldn't notice if her stupid body decided to betray her.

She unhooked her bike from the back of her car, tucked her ID card and a debit card into the little pack she had for the handlebars and then slid her water bottle into a holder on the frame of the bike.

Jake pulled in beside her just as she was pulling her hair up into a high ponytail that would keep it out of her face and off her neck.

"Hi," she said as he got out of his car.

"Hello, yourself. I see you made it."

Sporting the ubiquitous biker shorts and a nylon T-shirt, he looked totally as at home in this world as he did at the hospital. She couldn't believe she'd thought he was just starting out the other day when he arrived at the hospital. His helmet hung from the handlebars of his bike. Hmm… She'd brought one in her car, but Texas law had made bike helmets optional. This wasn't Austin, where she'd ridden mostly in designated bike areas, though, and she had no idea what the conditions would be. And when she looked around she saw the majority of other folks also had helmets.

That made her decision. She put down her kickstand and unlocked her car, pulling out the helmet. She'd have to readjust her hair to get the thing on, and she hated how hot it could be. But the others knew a thing or two about the road conditions in this part of the state. She would follow their lead. Of course everyone but her was in shorts, too, but that wasn't something she was likely to ever change.

"I did make it." She glanced around. "How many do you normally have ride with you?"

"Around fifteen or so. But for special events there might be forty."

"Wow. The club I was part of in Austin wasn't that large. But it wasn't organized by a bike shop, either, so maybe that's where the difference comes in."

"I think different clubs each have their own feel. This one is pretty laid-back." He nodded at someone who'd moved toward them. "Hi, Randy, how are you?"

He chatted with the other man for a minute before introducing them. "This is Elia. She's new to the area and thought she'd give the club a shot."

He smiled at her. "Well, we'll try not to scare you off, although if Jake hasn't already done that by now, then you should be good. He's the scariest one of all."

She could agree with that. Oh, not about the scary part, but about the scary reaction she had to him. It was kind of like when Matt had had that febrile reaction to his antibiotic. The man somehow made her feel feverish just by being in the vicinity. It was actually a relief to talk to someone else and get her mind off of it.

She decided to play it all off as a joke. "I work with him, so I'm used to him."

Not hardly, but she could pretend, right?

"Does anyone *ever* get used to Jakob Callin?" Randy asked.

Time for another quip. "I don't know. You tell me."

"I think it would take a rare individual."

Jake rolled his eyes, and those in the vicinity all laughed.

A few seconds later, more people gathered around and were chatting. These folks obviously had a good rapport and had done many rides together. It might be easy just to fall in with them, but she wasn't sure that was such a good idea. Maybe it would be better to try out one of the other shops and see what they had to offer. But it was nice to be included, even if it was because of her being Jake's "plus-one."

Except she wasn't really. She was just in his orbit for this one ride. And then she would pop right back out of it, if she knew what was good for her.

Glancing at her watch, she saw that it was eight o'clock on the dot.

As if reading her mind, Randy spoke up. "So it looks like Brian—our fearless bike store leader—put me in charge of today's ride, since he's in Florida on vacation. Anyone know if others are coming?"

At the shake of several heads, he rubbed his hands together. "Okay, let's gear up, then."

Elia followed their lead and adjusted her ponytail so it trailed down her back and slid her helmet on, buckling it in place. "How fast do you all ride?"

Randy evidently overheard her and said, "It's pretty much a set your own pace thing. It depends on what you're working toward. Some of us have races coming up. Some are just here for pleasure. If you drop out, though, please let someone know. Speaking of which, can I have your name and phone number?"

Out of the corner of her eye she saw Jake frown. But why? Was he afraid she'd start pushing her way into the group? If that was his worry, he needn't. She wasn't likely to try to stick around longer than this one ride. Maybe she should reassure him.

But that would be awkward.

She gave her name and cell number to Randy, and he put them into his phone. "If we lose each other, I'll text you to make sure all is well."

She glanced around. No one else seemed to think that was something out of the ordinary. Except Jake was still frowning.

How fast were they planning on riding? She leaned toward him. "Are you guys going to run thirty miles an hour or something?"

"No. Don't worry. I won't lose you."

The way he said it made her shiver, even though she knew he didn't mean any more by it than Randy had. And the inference that she might be the only one to fall behind should have irritated her, but it didn't. But it did spur her to make sure she held her own. No leisurely pedaling like she might have done in Austin, where her group was more about scenery than distance traveled.

"How do you know I won't lose you?"

He chuckled. "Is that a challenge?"

That made her gulp. "Actually no. The group I rode with did scenic rides with lots of chatting within the whole group. We pretty much stayed in a clump."

"I see. This group is a little more competitive than that, but it's definitely not a race. For most of us, at least. There are always one or two who like to be in the lead the whole way."

But evidently Jake was not one of those. And yet he led the way in the burn unit, and from what she'd heard he was one of the best reconstructive surgeons in the Dallas area. So he was certainly out in front. But maybe that wasn't about being competitive. She had a feeling he cared much more about his patients than he did about his rankings among other plastic surgeons.

They all got on their bikes and started off in a big group. Within a mile, though, it had spread out a little so they weren't all on top of each other. Jake stayed with her, and she hoped that wasn't just to be nice. She didn't want to hold him back if he wanted to go on ahead. But she liked the fact that he didn't feel the need to show off, either. Randy was definitely up ahead, although he wasn't the leader of the pack.

There were only two people that she saw who weren't wearing helmets. And probably 75 percent of the group were men. If she hadn't had her injury, would she have taken up biking as a competitive sport?

It was kind of a moot question, because she *had* been injured and cycling was one of the most comfortable ways she could think of to keep the range of motion in the leg as close to normal as she could.

"Is this a comfortable pace for you?" Jake's question made her wonder if he'd read her mind.

"This is good. It's a little faster than I normally go, but I'm definitely not having any problems keeping up." And it was true, she didn't even feel winded.

Jake pointed to the right. "We're in the neighborhood of University Park right now."

With its tall trees, manicured landscaping and dappled bike path, it wasn't the concrete jungle she'd always pictured Dallas as. "It's a pretty area."

"It is. It's one of the shadier areas on our route. It'll be a lot warmer around the airport. But we should be done around noonish or a little before, so definitely before the heat of the day sets in."

They started to go down a long hill and Elia stopped pedaling, adding a little brake when her speed picked up. "I guess I should have asked about the topography. Are we in for some steep inclines?"

"Not super steep, but we will start climbing at around the ten-mile mark, where we'll stay until mile twenty-five-ish, where we'll start back down. The rest of the ride will be pretty flat. How were the rides in Austin?"

"Austin is in hill country and most of our rides end up going downhill first—since Austin itself is higher than the surrounding areas—and then climbing to get back to our starting point."

Steep climbs were the only things she found difficult in cycling. For some of it she had to rise out of her seat to pedal, and that required her right leg to straighten to the point that she felt a sharp pull behind her knee from the con- tracted tissue. She could do it, but normally ended up having to go home and ice the back of her leg. She was wary of using more pain- killers than absolutely necessary. She glanced over at him. This was probably the most re- laxed she'd ever seen Jake. He definitely liked coming out and riding. And he looked far too good for comfort as he leaned over the handle- bars. He had the proportions of a cyclist, the snug athletic shirt showing off the long line of his back to perfection. And the muscles in his calves…

She turned her attention back to the road in a hurry. Time to occupy her thoughts with something else. "Are you the one who came up with the idea for the bike festival?"

"No, actually, it's been around for quite a while. But when I came to the hospital, I was already a cyclist so it fit in with who I am. I haven't missed a year yet."

"It's just a little different. I normally see hospitals doing marathons or the like."

"There's nothing wrong with being a little different."

She would agree with him, although there was a time when she'd felt so different from everyone else that she struggled with anxiety. She'd gotten counseling as a teen that had helped her realize that her burns made her more empathetic to those with challenges. In Austin, she'd helped with the Special Olympics in the area and had loved being a part of something so affirming.

"No. There's not." She said it because it was what was expected of her, but realized she'd actually come to believe it.

"We're coming up to a busier area, so we'll have some traffic lights to contend with. And the path will merge onto the road as part of the far right lane."

Just like he'd said, she saw the first major intersection of the trip was up ahead. Traffic next to the bike path was picking up, as well. And within fifty yards, the path veered onto the street, where a marked-off section identified it with a bike symbol painted on the asphalt.

They stopped for the light, catching up with a big part of their group, the ones who'd lagged behind reappearing and joining them. The light turned green. She put her foot on the pedal and pushed off, only to hear a shout, then Jake's hand reached over and grabbed her handlebars, pulling hard and knocking them both off balance. The pavement came up to meet her, and she heard the squeal of tires. She braced for what she thought was coming, but shockingly nothing hit her or ran over her. But she did hear a scream from someone, and Jake, who was on the ground beside her, leaped to his feet, glancing at her. "You okay?"

"Yes, I think so."

She still didn't understand exactly what had happened until she started to climb to her feet and her eyes caught on the sight of a car who'd hit a nearby tree. And under its tires was a dark blue bike. And the rider... She used her hands to shield her eyes from the sun as Jake and some others ran to an area beside the tree, where a figure lay in the grass, looking far too still.

CHAPTER FOUR

JAKE GOT TO the cyclist's side first and saw it was Randy. Hell! And he wasn't moving. At all.

His helmet was in place but blood was pooled on the ground next to him, looking like it was coming from his nose. Kneeling beside him, he felt for a pulse. It was there, but thready.

If he hadn't jerked on Elia's handlebars, they would have been hit, as well. His knees were stinging as was one of his elbows, but those were the least of his worries.

As if summoned, Elia appeared beside him, squatting in the grass next to him. "God. He's been thrown at least twenty yards. Pulse?"

"Yes. But there's a good chance there's some internal bleeding going on."

One of Randy's arms was bent at the elbow, but the bend went the wrong way. Fracture number one. And there were probably more where that came from. Damn, who in their right mind flew through an intersection like that?

Another of their group came up beside them. "EMTs are on their way. I can't even believe this happened. What was that driver thinking?"

"I have no idea, Serge, but thanks for calling it in. We're not going to move him until the squad gets here." There was no telling if his spine or neck were included in his injuries, but moving Randy could prove catastrophic if there were broken vertebrae involved. "Anyone else hurt?"

Serge shook his head. "No. But if you hadn't purposely crashed your bikes, you undoubtedly would have been hit, too."

He hadn't meant to hurt Elia, but it was either that or chance them both being struck by the car.

When he glanced at her, he noted there was blood on her cheek from a scrape and her bottom lip was also bloody and already swelling. But she seemed okay. "Can you check on the driver?"

"Sure thing."

She got up and disappeared from sight only to come back a few minutes later. "He's out of the car, sitting on the curb. Appears uninjured. But I got a strong whiff of alcohol on his breath, although he denies he's been drinking. And he hasn't asked about whether or not anyone was hurt. He seems totally out of it, so there may be something besides alcohol in his system."

Damn it. The way the guy had come flying down that road, Jake had known he wasn't going to try to stop for the light. And he'd been right. He couldn't believe there weren't more injuries. In the distance he could hear the sound of sirens. Finally!

A police car was the first on the scene. He started to get up, but Elia shook her head. "You stay with Randy, and I'll go talk to him."

Just then, the man groaned and his eyes opened. But when he went to move his injured arm, Jake stopped him. "Just lay still for a minute, buddy, until they can get you checked out." Jake didn't want to upset the man who prided himself on how healthy he was and how infrequently he visited his family doctor—whom he thought might even be retired. But there was no way healthy living was going to fix this. Not without some help.

He was vaguely aware of the police ushering the driver of the car into the back of their cruiser. Thank God. At least he wouldn't be behind the wheel again today to hurt or kill someone else. The other people of their party were asking about Randy and more onlookers were gathering, so he told those from the bike club what he could but suggested they all either continue on with the ride or head home. He would let them know what he could, if Randy said it was okay. He was still pretty sure the man had more going on than a broken arm. His belly felt taut in a way that was more than just muscle. He needed to be transported and soon.

The band of riders headed off, and the other sirens got increasingly louder. This time they were who he was looking for. At that moment Elia came back over. "How's he doing now?"

"I'll feel a hell of a lot better when he's en route to the hospital. I think he's got some bleeding going on in his belly, and his arm is a mess. He'll need surgery for sure. And there's no telling about his neck or back."

Randy was in and out of it, coherent one minute and unconscious the next. But maybe that was better.

Jake glanced at Elia and saw it wasn't just her cheek and her lip that were injured. She had holes torn in both of the knees of her Lycra pants, and they were covered in congealed blood from where they'd skidded on the pavement. And she held her right arm across her belly, something he hadn't noted earlier. "What's going on with you? Are you hurt?" He reached up to move her arm so he could see, and she winced.

"I think I just sprained my wrist. It's fine. What can I do?"

He studied her face for a second before saying, "I think EMTs are almost here. So just help me keep him still if he starts thrashing around."

Thankfully he didn't, and in a few minutes, Randy had been fitted with a cervical collar and was loaded onto a backboard. Westlake was too far, so they were going to take him to an area hospital that was closer. But at least he was stable for the moment.

There was a second squad and Jake tried to get Elia to get herself checked out, but she refused. "I'm fine. Really. I just want to get home so I can get cleaned up."

"I don't think you should ride with that hand." He looked over at where other bike club members had dragged their two bikes from the road once the police had finished taking pictures of the scene. His looked okay, but

Elia's… "And I don't think your bike is road-worthy right now."

The gear shifting mechanism was hanging off the handlebars, connected only by a wire.

"Oh, no." Then she chuckled. "Well, at least I know where a good bike repair place is."

He thought for a minute. "I only live a few minutes from here. If you're up to walking we could wheel the bikes there, and you could get cleaned up a little. How bad is your hand?"

"Definitely not broken. Just sore. I should be able to wheel my bike. I could do with some Tylenol, though, so if you have some, I'll take you up on your offer. My house is a lot further away, and our cars are still at the bike shop."

"I have Tylenol."

All the spectators had left the area, and it was eerily quiet. The drunk's car was still where it had crashed, and he assumed the police would impound it as evidence.

He picked up her bike and wheeled it a few paces to make sure it still rolled freely, then handed it to her. "Are you sure you can do it? I could lock my bike up someplace and come back for it later."

"Your bike is a lot fancier than mine. More chances of someone coming along and breaking the chain. Besides, I can do it."

"I'm about a fifteen-minute walk. Are you sure? I could always ride back to the bike shop and drive your car back."

She gave a visible shiver. "If you're okay with it, I think it would be faster just to walk to your place."

How much pain was she in? "Is the Tylenol for your hand?"

She hesitated. "Not specifically. Just sore and achy and I have a slight headache."

Putting her kickstand down, he came over and tipped up her chin, checking her pupils. They were even and he could see them both reacting to light when he turned her toward the sun. His eyes perused her face, skimming over it, his thumb touching the area of the cut on her lip before he could stop himself. "Hurt?"

She pulled away with a slight smile. "No to the brain bleed. And yes to the lip. It stings, but nothing major."

Hell. What was he thinking? He was glad she pulled away, because for a second the impulse to lean over and kiss the bruise on her mouth had stolen over him. That would be a little harder to blow off as simple concern for her well-being. And he hadn't been lying about office romances being messy.

His ex hadn't worked at the hospital, but

their breakup had not been fun. She'd gone on a rant on social media about him, tagging him in a post that he'd only seen weeks later, when his mom had called him asking what was going on. He rarely went on those sites, despite having opened a profile. In fact, he'd only done so because his mom had asked him to, saying she wanted to be able to keep up with what was going on in his life. He didn't think seeing him blasted by someone who was in the public eye was quite what she had in mind. His mom had had to tell him how to take the tag off and unfriend Samantha. But not before he'd noted that there were thousands of comments from her fans lambasting him for something he hadn't done.

"I'll give you some Tylenol, but if your headache gets worse—"

"*Deus!* I'm a nurse, Jake, remember? You don't think I know the signs?" As if realizing how vehement she'd sounded, she quickly added, "I'm sorry. It's just a little embarrassing standing here with my clothes the way they are. Your shirt is ripped, as well."

Was it? He glanced at his shoulder, which had just started to ache, and saw that his shirt was indeed torn at the seam, his sleeve hanging halfway down his arm. "So it is. Okay, are you ready?"

"I am. Which direction?"

"Back the way we came." He picked up his bike and waited for her to join him.

Their helmets were both off by now, so they buckled them around their handlebars. He'd need to remind himself to replace his before his next ride since they'd fallen and there could be unseen damage to the protective gear.

They started walking and Jake quickly saw Elia's limp was more pronounced than it usually was. He'd never asked her about the slight hitch in her step, figuring that if she wanted to tell him she would. She still said nothing, but within five minutes the tense set of her mouth was unmistakable.

"Did you injure your leg?"

"Just strained an old injury. I'll be fine. I just need a painkiller."

He assumed she was talking about the Tylenol. They could try to hail a cab, but in this part of town they weren't as common as they were near the airport itself. "We have about seven more minutes or so to go. Are you sure you want to keep walking?"

"Yes. I can make it. Once I get off it and take something, it'll be as good as new."

He doubted that, but unless he wanted to challenge her or ask exactly what the injury was, he was stuck taking her at her word. But he could at least try. "Anything you want to talk about?"

Her head jerked to look at him before turning back to the road. "Nope. It's not important."

Except he felt like it was. At least to her.

He slowed his pace twice to accommodate her increasing signs of discomfort and the fact that she was now leaning on her bike for support. Thankfully his apartment complex was just on the next block.

Two minutes later they were there. He helped her connect her bike to the stand that was at the front entryway, while opting to take his own upstairs. The look of relief on her face at not having to push it anymore was obvious. He'd made the right choice.

"Do you want to lean on me?"

"No. I've got it, but thanks."

The elevator was oversize, one of the features he'd liked about the place when he'd looked at it several years ago, and he hadn't regretted the decision. Located in a quiet suburb of northwest Dallas, it was both close to his job and within a reasonable distance to the airport, when he wanted to visit his mom who'd chosen to move to Florida a few years after his dad passed away from cancer.

He unlocked his door and ushered her inside. "Why don't you sit on the couch and I'll get you that Tylenol."

When she didn't argue, just headed over to the couch, using her good hand to help lower herself onto it, he knew she was more uncomfortable than she'd been willing to say. And stubborn, for sure.

He hung his bike on a pulley system he'd rigged from the ceiling and hoisted it up out of the way and then went into the kitchen for the painkillers and a glass of water. Handing it to her, she downed both the pills in one gulp. "Thanks."

She reconfigured her ponytail so that it was up off her neck the way it had been when she'd first arrived at the bike shop. "Do you mind if I take off my shoes?"

"No, of course not."

She toed off her tennis shoes and made circles with her right foot. Had she sprained that one, as well? Or maybe that's where her old injury had been, although he didn't think so. It looked to be more around the knee area, although there was no way to know for sure, since she hadn't said anything about it.

"I have some bike shorts that I think might fit you…or at least not fall off of you."

She was quick to shake her head. "But if you have some sweats that I can snug up around my waist, I'll accept that, though."

Sweats would be horribly hot this time of day, but he sensed it was the shorts she had an issue with. She could have a surgical scar or even a port-wine stain that she was self-conscious about. It would explain the longer gear she'd worn today. "I have some running pants that are lighter weight and have a drawstring waist, if that would work."

She looked grateful. "Yes, that would be perfect, thanks. Can I wait until the Tylenol kicks in before moving off the couch? I know I'm imposing—"

"You're not imposing at all. How about some tea or coffee?"

"I'd love some strong coffee if it's not a problem."

"Not at all."

He made a cup and carried it out to her along with some sugar packets and a carton of creamer. She murmured her thanks and took a sip, leaning back with a sigh. "Perfect, thanks so much. As soon as the painkillers hit my system, I'll call a cab and be out of your hair."

"There's no hurry. I had no plans for today other than that ride. Will you be okay if I take a quick shower?" He paused. "Unless you want to go first? Then I'll call and check on Randy."

"No. Take your time. I'm just going to enjoy this coffee and being off my feet."

"Do you want ice or a heating pad?"

"No. I'm good. Go get your shower."

She did seem more relaxed than she'd been moments earlier, so maybe just sitting down had helped ease whatever was hurting. "I won't be long."

Leaving her, he headed back to his bedroom, pulling out clothes for himself and then finding a T-shirt and a pair of his running pants that he used for sleepwear in his bottom drawer. Then, taking them all into the bathroom, he laid hers on a section of counter next to the sink and turned on the water.

Her leg hurt like fire and the neuralgia in her foot had kicked into high gear, the combination making it difficult to walk without gritting her teeth. It felt so much better to be sitting, where she could keep her leg bent at an angle where the inflammation wouldn't kick her butt.

Jake had looked at her funny when she refused his offer of biking shorts. But covering up her scars had become such a way of life that the thought of him seeing them or going out of the apartment complex with them on display made her break out in a cold sweat.

Her cellphone pinged and she glanced at it. It was her mom.

How was the ride today?

Thank God her mom hadn't yet heard the news about the accident, although she was pretty sure it would be on the internet somewhere by now. So how to answer without making her worried sick or having her rush to Dallas to check on her in person?

She composed her words carefully.

We ended up stopping early because of some traffic problems, but the beginning of it was good. Everyone was nice and helpful.

There. It was all true, even if she had definitely played down their reasons for stopping.

She could still hear the water running in the bathroom. It was somehow soothing to know Jake was in there. If she'd been by herself today, she wasn't sure what she would have done. Someone would have probably helped her get home, but it had been nice to have someone actually there while she walked in case she hadn't been able to go any farther.

Her eyes trailed around the room as she waited for her mom to respond. Jake's place was kind of a minimalist's haven. She was pretty sure it wasn't so much due to preference as it was the fact that he lived alone and was at work most days. Like her own apartment, it was probably just a place to sleep before returning to the hospital.

I'm glad. We're thinking of coming up to see you next weekend, if that's okay? I'm planning on making more of your bike cookies to bring with me.

Thank God they weren't on their way now, like they'd often done in the past, just showing up on her doorstep. Elia definitely wouldn't want them to see her like this.

Thank you so much. That sounds perfect! Talk soon. Love you both!

The sound of running water stopped, and Elia took a couple more sips of her coffee, which was still piping hot. Jake hadn't been kidding about being quick.

What else was the man quick about?

Her eyes immediately widened and her face heated. What on earth had made her think of that? Maybe the fact that she was uncomfortably aware that he was naked in that room.

Well, you'd better wipe those thoughts from your head, right now.

Within thirty seconds, he'd rejoined her, his hair wet and slicked back, making a few strands of gray stand out against the thick darker locks. He was dressed in jeans and a muscle shirt that made her swallow and sent her thoughts flying back in the wrong direction. It didn't help that the scents of soap and a clean body followed him into the space, making her want to trap them deep in her lungs.

For what purpose?

She doubted she would ever be in the room with a freshly showered Jake ever again, so why not enjoy a little guilty pleasure. Like the hint of muscle that rippled in his biceps when he picked up her tray and asked if she wanted more coffee.

"No, thanks. I'm good. The Tylenol is already kicking in. Do you mind if I shower, too? I'm a mess and would love to wash some of this gunk from my knees and face before I head home."

"I thought you might want to. I left some clothes in there and there's shampoo and soap in the shower. And Band-Aids and antibiotic cream in the medicine cabinet on the wall."

"Thanks." Now, if she could just get to her feet without groaning... Although she hadn't been lying. The Tylenol was hitting her system with a relief that let her breathe again.

He reached down his hand, and this time she accepted the offer of help, somehow levering herself to her feet without an audible sound. At least she hoped not, because the warmth of the hand encasing hers sent a shiver through her that she felt with her whole being.

She limped into the bathroom and was once again surrounded by the scent of Jake. The moist humid air was the same air that had washed over him just a few moments earlier. Another shiver went through her, as well as a rush of heat that centered in her belly and traveled lower. She swallowed, trying to lose the sensation.

Failing that, she used her hand to wipe clear a spot in the fogged-up mirror and leaned forward to look at her face.

Wow. She hadn't been kidding. She really

was a mess. Her hair was sticking out in all directions and a part of it was matted with what she could only guess was blood from her scraped cheek. Raising her fingers to touch it, she winced. It was raw and red, and by tomorrow would almost surely be a bruise.

And her lip was also swollen. When he had grabbed her bike and she realized she was going to fall, a shard of sheer anger had gone through her. Until she heard the screech of tires and understood why he'd done what he had. He may very well have saved her life. And when his thumb had touched the injury on her mouth...

She'd jerked away out of self-preservation. Because the sensation of his skin sliding against hers was the sort of thing dreams were made of. Just like when he'd touched her hand.

Pulling in a deep breath, she exhaled and told herself to get her act together. She yanked her shirt over her head and rolled her shoulders, trying to slough off the tension she'd carried all the way up to his apartment. Unclasping her bra and letting it drop on the floor with her top, she set about unrolling her Lycra bike pants down her hips and easing them away from her skinned knees. Once they were off, she turned her scarred leg and craned her neck to see the back of it, where the patchy sections of what were once skin grafts had changed to a ropey tight mass of scar tissue that prevented her from straightening her leg completely. Other than her knees, there weren't any visible injuries, but that leg hurt worse than it had in a very long time. She could only assume that in the fall it had straightened past its limits and had torn some of the adhesions on the inside.

In her normal, everyday life, she tried not to look at her leg that much. It got her to where she was going and she convinced herself that that was all that mattered. Except on rare occasions when someone made her feel self-conscious about it, like the man who'd liked to keep the covers pulled up. But that was years ago, and she would have thought she would have gotten over all of that by now. But picturing Jake, with his perfect smooth limbs that rippled with muscle, had brought it all back again. She'd been horrified at the thought of wearing shorts in front of him. And it made her angry.

She'd cared for people who had burns in very visible places. People who were missing parts of their face or who had scars that couldn't be eradicated with surgery. Places they didn't have the luxury of hiding. And here she was moaning to herself about scars that most people didn't even realize existed.

Get over yourself, Elia. Seriously. Start realizing how fortunate you are.

She turned away from the mirror and went over to the shower, which was actually part of a deep soaking tub. She stared at it for a second. The heat of that would really do her muscles some good. Surely he wouldn't mind…

Stepping under the spray of the shower, she let warm water sluice over her face and knees to wash away the blood, wincing as it hit the scraped flesh. Then she washed her hair using his shampoo, giving herself permission to submerge her senses in something he'd chosen. After all, he'd offered it up to her. And he would never know how it made her feel…right?

Then she turned off the shower feature, pushed a button to stop the water from draining and lowered herself into the tub, adjusting the dials so that the water was much warmer than the shower had been. As the silky liquid covered her calves and then her shins, she reached up and squeezed a little of his shampoo beneath the spigot so that it made a scented froth of bubbles before putting the bottle back and leaning against the backrest.

Closing her eyes, she sighed as the water trailed over her thighs and slid between them, reaching sensitive areas that hadn't been touched in quite a while. She bit her lip, before the sting of the injury on it made her release it quickly. But still, she let herself enjoy the sensations of the warm bath flowing over her belly and up her torso. The heat was already easing the neuralgia in her foot while igniting nerve endings in other places that felt a whole lot better than the pins-and-needles prickling she lived with on a daily basis.

It reached the bottom of her breasts and she held her breath as it slowly worked its way higher, like the teasing fingers of a lover. An image flickered between her closed lids, and although she tried to keep the features from sharpening into something recognizable, she failed. And just as the water reached her nipples and surrounded them with moist heat, she gave in to the temptation and let her hands go up and slide over them, moaning softly as they came to instant life.

She leaned forward enough to turn off the water before sinking back into it and continuing her fantasy. The one where Jake's hands were the ones covering her breasts, his palms massaging and coaxing them to pucker against his skin. She swallowed, trying to banish the sensations. Until, in her head, his mouth covered one… She arched toward the imaginary figure, while her other hand touched her belly, slowly moving down to where a growing need was whispering for her to give in. To give it what it wanted. The fantasy. The unreachable reality of what might have been.

The second she reached lower, the pulsing need grew out of control. It couldn't be stopped. Wouldn't be. Her breathing grew ragged as she let herself climb that hill. As she got closer and closer to what her body needed. Something that would obliterate the pain in her leg. At least for a few minutes.

Her fingers quickened in time with the beat of her heart. So close…

So…very…close…

Her brain froze as sheer pleasure washed over her, her hips arching up and seeking something…

Something that wasn't there.

She came down quicker than she expected, sinking back into the water in instant dismay. She couldn't believe she'd done that. In Jake's bathroom, of all places!

And now she was going to have to climb out

of his tub and step into his clothes, and then walk out there and face him.

The man she'd just imagined having sex with!

God! If she could pull on her ratty, torn bike pants and shirt without him questioning why she hadn't used his clothes, she would. But of course he would ask. And she wasn't about to tell him the reason.

So she finished washing and quickly drained the tub, rinsing out any evidence of her illicit bubble bath. Suddenly shivering, she wrapped herself in the thick bath towel he'd left for her and patted herself dry, putting her panties and bra back on. She hesitated for a long time over the clothing folded on the countertop before her shoulders slumped and she reached for them, pulling the T-shirt over her head and letting the fabric fall. It came down to mid-thigh, making her smile for a second before it disappeared again. Then she pulled on the lightweight jogging pants, cinching them around her waist. It felt intimate. Almost as intimate as what she'd done in that tub.

But he was never going to know about that. Not if she could help it.

Gathering her clothes and glancing at her

face one last time to make sure there was no sign of guilt—at least no visible sign—she turned the handle and walked out of the bathroom.

CHAPTER FIVE

SHE CAME OUT of the bathroom, her wet hair wonderfully mussed and her face pink with the heat of her shower. And hell if she didn't look sexy as anything in his clothes. The words he'd planned to say when she emerged curled around his tongue and got stuck for a moment before he finally got them out.

"Randy's okay. I called the hospital. A broken rib hit a blood vessel and needed to be cauterized and the ends of the bone wired back together, but no damage to his spleen or other internal organs. His arm is splinted, but he'll probably need another surgery because of where the break occurred, but it could have been much worse."

"Much worse," she echoed in a weird voice.

"Are you okay? Is the pain worse?" He studied her face. The blood was gone, but her cheek was already turning colors. He wouldn't be surprised if she had a black eye by morning.

"No. The water helped actually. Thanks for letting me use your bathroom. And your clothes." She glanced down at herself.

Her face seemed to turn a darker shade of red, which he didn't understand. Unless she was embarrassed about having to borrow his clothes. It wasn't a big deal. Or maybe she was just anxious to be on her way so she could relax in her own space.

"I had a thought. It won't take me terribly long to ride to the bike shop. Maybe a half hour, tops. I could pick up my car, drive home and then drive you and your bike to the shop to get your car."

She seemed to think about it for a minute. "I was going to suggest I just call a taxi service, but then you'd be stuck with my bike until I could come back and pick it up. Are sure you don't mind?"

"I think it's the most logical course of action. And your bike is out of commission. The shop might still be open and you could leave it there for repairs."

"Okay, that sounds like a plan. Thanks for doing that." She gave a wry twist of her mouth. "It seems I have a lot to thank you for. I never thought I'd be thanking someone for knocking me off my bike, but you probably saved me from being hit along with Randy. I had no idea that car was even coming."

"No need for thanks. And I only just happened to look again as we were crossing the street and caught movement out of the corner of my eye." He grinned. "And I never thought I'd be the one who'd cause a fellow biker to fall. On purpose."

"You saved my life." Her voice held a hint of shakiness that took him by surprise.

He went over and tipped up her chin like he had at the scene of the accident. "We might not have ended up in the danger zone even if I hadn't grabbed your handlebars, but I couldn't take that chance. Even if I'd shouted your name, by the time you had a chance to look it would have been too late."

"Well, thank you, anyway."

His eyes went to her lips and the impulse to kiss her was strong. Strong enough that he allowed himself to lean forward, but only to give her a quick peck on the nose. "I'm glad you're okay. Headache gone?"

"Yes. It must have been…er, those pain relievers I took." She took a step back, and he realized he still had his fingers tucked under her chin.

Hell, the fall must have knocked something loose in his head. Something important.

He forced himself to go over and lower his bike from its spot against the ceiling and set the kickstand. "Do you want something to eat before I go? More coffee?"

"No, I'll be okay, thanks."

"All right. I'll be back as soon as I can, barring any problems. And I'll text you if that happens."

She nodded. "Thanks again."

"Make yourself at home while I'm gone. There's stuff in the fridge and a French press coffee maker on the counter." He wheeled his bike to the door and went through, taking the elevator back down to the ground floor.

Getting on, he started pedaling as if his life depended on it. He'd almost kissed her. Really kissed her and not just on the nose. After the accident, when he was trying to assess Randy's injuries, it had gone through his head that it could have been not only Randy, but Elia flung across the road like a rag doll. It could be her with broken limbs...or worse.

But kissing her? Not in the cards. Not for him. He didn't do relationships. At least not right now. He did not want another Samantha-like situation to contend with. He really was pretty happy with living by himself. At thirty-eight, he was pretty much used to being alone and childless. It suited him. He kept terrible hours and was at the hospital most of the time. His apartment was really just a park-for-the-night place that held no real significance for him. It could have been anywhere and it would have been exactly the same.

So no, he didn't want to start something with her, even if she were interested, which he was pretty sure she wasn't. She'd acted a little odd being in his apartment, and it was probably that she was thinking the same thing…that she hoped he wasn't going to hit on her.

And then he had to go and tilt her face up and give her a peck on the nose.

A friend would have done the same, right? Had he ever kissed a friend on the nose before?

No. But he didn't have very many female friends. And he didn't really know her well enough to consider her a friend.

And maybe it was best to keep it that way. She was a colleague and could stay in that category. No jumping lanes. No getting to know her on a more intimate level…even if he was physically attracted to her. And he wouldn't deny that he was, because Jake didn't make it a habit to lie and that would be lying to himself.

So yes, she was a gorgeous, smart, interesting woman who had secrets he'd like to uncover. But he wouldn't pry. Wouldn't probe. Because if he did, he'd be in danger of getting a little deeper than he intended to get.

So as soon as he took her home, he was going to try to not have much contact with her outside of work. And hopefully, she wouldn't be interested in joining his bike club on more rides like the one today.

Even if there were no more accidents. Physical or otherwise. Because if he kept socializing with her on a casual basis, there was every chance that something not so casual might happen. And that might just upset everything in the little "bachelor forever" pep talk he'd just given himself.

Something he didn't want to happen.

Now…or any time in the near future.

Matt's first skin graft was today. Over the last week, they'd completed the bone grafts for his jaw, and those seemed to be taking without a problem. The tooth implant surgery was coming in the near future, but it was time to start building the scaffolding from the skin cells they would harvest from Matt's clavicle area, which was one of the areas that best matched the skin tones of the face. And Jake had chosen to do a sheet graph—using the skin just as it was harvested rather than running it through a mesh machine, which would thin the layer of skin and allow it to cover a larger area. But the meshed skin would also be more likely to scar, something he didn't want to risk on Matt's face. And there'd be enough tissue to do the job without needing to resort to that.

Randy was home from the hospital as of two days ago. Jake had checked on him daily, and when he'd seen Elia over the normal course of the day at the hospital, he'd relayed the news, but he hadn't spoken to her any more than necessary. And she'd assured him that her leg was better and that her bike had already been repaired and all was well.

Her cheek, which had appeared bruised for the first couple of days, now showed no signs of what had happened. Neither did her lip, which was once again smooth and silky looking.

And those bike cookies kept on coming. And the list of people attending the fundraiser kept getting longer. It looked like it was going to be a record turnout, if the statistics were anything to go by.

He headed down the hallway, bypassing

the jar of cookies, to Matt's room to see how he was doing mentally before they got him prepped for surgery.

Pushing the door open, he gave an inward groan. Elia was in the room, getting his vitals and chitchatting with the patient and his parents as if she were perfectly at ease, something she didn't display around him. Instead, she still seemed vaguely uptight, although she did a good job hiding it with a cheery greeting and smile.

Should he apologize for what had happened in his apartment?

Except it wasn't like they'd had sex. But she might not have welcomed that quick display of relief that she was okay.

So yes. An apology might be in order. If she indicated it was no big deal, they could go on about their lives as if nothing had happened. And if not, then at least she would know that he was truly sorry to have done anything to make her uncomfortable.

She turned and saw him and her smile caved in, becoming the very picture of an efficient nurse. Not that she hadn't had that image before. But she seemed determined not to let him see any other side of her.

And he couldn't blame her.

Jake greeted Matt's parents, shaking both of their hands before Elia recited his vitals—everything looked great—then she asked when they were coming to get him ready for surgery.

"Pretty quickly, I would guess. Surgery is scheduled for ten this morning." A little more than an hour away. He would be heading there to make his own preparations soon.

"How long do you expect it to take?"

Okay, so she wasn't just answering him with monosyllabic replies. She was actually inviting a give-and-take of information. But probably for Matt's folks' sakes, since they were hanging on her every word. He decided to address them instead.

"About an hour and a half, although I have the surgical suite reserved for a two-hour block, just in case we run into any snags."

He turned back to Elia. "You're welcome to observe, if you'd like."

Matt's voice came from across the room. "Would you? It would make me feel better to know you're there. Kind of like a guardian angel, since you've helped us so much over these last couple of days, including recommending a counselor. I think Gracie, my parents and I are going to talk to her together. Gracie said you talked to her and helped her understand what it's like to be burned, since it happened to you, too."

Jake's brain seized for a second or two.

Burned? Elia had been burned? He turned to look at her in a hurry.

Her face flushed dark red, and she didn't say anything for a few seconds, then she just murmured, "I'm glad it helped, although it was a long time ago. But yes, I'll observe the procedure if it helps you feel more comfortable."

Matt's mom went over and gave Elia a long hug before releasing her with tears in her eyes. "Thank you so much. For everything. Especially talking to Gracie."

Jake glanced at her leg and suddenly things seemed to fall into place. She'd said she'd aggravated an old injury when asked why she was limping after falling off her bike. But he'd assumed she'd broken a bone or had some other type of injury to the limb. But what if it wasn't?

Maybe her reasons for working in a burn unit were much more personal than he'd imagined. If so, he completely understood that feeling. Wasn't he working here because of what he'd seen? Oh, he hadn't personally been burned. But the pilot who'd been injured had somehow changed his heart, nudging it to go in a different direction than he'd intended to go. He'd always had his heart set on being a plastic surgeon, but that pilot was the reason that he'd specialized in skin grafting and reconstruction.

Regardless of whether she'd received an injury a long time ago or not, that didn't change the fact that he needed to at least offer an apology. Now more than ever.

She looked at him, her chin held slightly higher than it had been before, as if daring him to ask her about what had happened. He wouldn't. At least not here in front of a patient. "Where is the observation area?" she asked.

"We'll be in surgical suite number four. The viewing room just above it was put in for students to observe specific procedures that go along with their curriculum. But there shouldn't be any students at this point in time, since it's summer. Maybe one or two who have some makeup work to do, but otherwise you should pretty much have the space to yourself."

"Okay, thanks for letting me watch."

Matt nodded. "I'm really grateful. Gracie will feel better, too." The teen's speech was a little difficult to understand, since his lower jaw was immobilized at the moment to help the bone grafts heal without putting any stress on them. But he was able to get his point across since he still had the use of his lips and tongue.

"I'm happy to do it. Although I'm sure everything will go just fine. Dr. Callin is a great surgeon. You'll be in good hands."

Even though it was a normal "nurse" thing to say to a patient, it still warmed him to hear the words. Even if they really weren't sincere.

She threw Matt's family a smile and turned to leave, but Jake stopped her with a touch to her arm. "Do you have a second?"

Her tongue snaked out to touch her lip, moistening it before she answered. "Sure. How about if I meet you outside."

She slid quietly through the door. Jake stayed for a moment or two longer to give some last-minute scheduling information to his patient and his parents about what to expect after Matt came out of surgery. Then he said his goodbyes, as well.

Elia leaned against the wall outside of Matt's room and closed her eyes for a second. It had been bound to get out, but for some reason she'd rather Jake not know about what happened to her. She hated feeling vulnerable, and having him know about her injury put her squarely in that position. She was normally pretty careful about who she gave that information to, figuring it was really no one's business. But on the other hand, she'd gone into this specialty because she thought she might be able to empathize with her patients better, since she knew exactly what it was like to go through painful procedures like debridement and surgeries. Matt was case in point.

Jake obviously wanted to talk about what he'd just learned, and she mentally tried to scale the information down to the size of a sound bite. Raw information with no commentary to go with it. She'd burned her leg as a child. It was now fine.

Unless he'd somehow guessed what she'd done in his bathroom and wanted to talk to her about that, rather than her leg.

No, that wasn't possible, unless he'd stood outside the door and put his ear to it to eavesdrop, and that would be a very creepy thing. Something she instinctively knew Jake wouldn't do.

Was it any creepier than pleasuring herself in his bathtub?

Deus! She still couldn't think about that without feeling mortified by her behavior.

But no…there was no way he knew about that, so it had to be about her leg.

She sensed more than heard the whisper of the door as it opened and shut, felt the slight breeze as the displaced air whispered across her cheek. She opened her eyes and found him looking at her.

"Not here," he said. "Can we walk outside for about five minutes?"

"Yep. I'm due for a break, anyway." Swallowing, she walked over to the nurse's station, where Sheryll was clacking away at the keys of the computer station. She glanced up, then looked at her over the top of her reading glasses.

She took a deep breath. "Can I run on break for a few minutes?"

"Of course." The nurse looked behind her and obviously noticed Jake standing there. Her eyes widened slightly, although she didn't say anything about that, just added, "Take as long as you need."

"Thanks. And actually Matt—our teen who's having surgery today—wants me to observe the operation. It'll probably be a couple of hours long. I'll completely understand if you can't spare me—"

"We'll be fine. You're off in an hour, anyway. Why don't you just go now. Norma should be here any minute."

"Are you sure?"

"Absolutely. I'll see you… Monday? Your folks are coming in tomorrow, aren't they?"

"Yes." She hadn't forgotten. Her mom and dad were both driving up, and while she was looking forward to seeing them, she didn't want them asking a lot of probing questions about the people she worked with. Ugh. Which might happen, despite the fact that her mom said it was about bringing up more cookies for the fundraiser. Things were getting more and more complicated.

The complicated part was on her end, though.

She was probably the one who was making things weird by keeping her old injury kind of a secret. It shouldn't be. Nor should she be self-conscious about it after all of these years.

She smiled at Sheryll. "Thank you again. Have a good weekend."

"I plan to. Hubs and I are headed to Lake Granbury for the weekend."

"Have fun! See you on Monday."

They didn't always get the whole weekend off, since the department still had to be staffed, but it had been a while since her friend had taken any personal time off.

Taking a deep breath, she turned back to Jake, wishing she'd told him she'd meet him outside rather than having to walk out of the building with him beside her. It made it look like they were fraternizing when they weren't at all.

She followed him out the nearest exit, which dumped them onto one of the hospital court-yards that attached to the Mocha Café by an-other door.

As soon as they reached a bench, she dropped onto it and waited for him to join her before turning his way. "Before you say anything, it's not something I normally talk about. I fell into a campfire when I was a child and burned my leg and part of my back. It happened so long ago and I've lived with it for so long, that it's not something I really dwell on."

He stared at her for a long moment before saying, "God, Elia, I'm sorry. That's not what I wanted to talk to you about, but I had no idea. It still bothers you after all this time?"

That wasn't why he'd wanted to speak to her? Then what was it?

She swallowed. "I wouldn't say 'bother,' per se. The scarring on my leg contracted across the back of my knee, creating a kind of sling-shot effect where I'm about ten degrees from being able to straighten my knee completely before the pull of the contracture becomes too much."

"Revision surgery didn't help?"

"No. My doctor tried twice to redo it. But I have keloid disorder, which complicated my recovery from the burns. And yes, after the revision surgeries they tried cortisone shots and pressure dressings to try to prevent the scars from going crazy again with the granulation tissue, but it didn't seem to help. I have a scar on my collarbone that also developed a keloid. Not a huge one, but it's still bigger than a simple scar."

He nodded. "Keloid disorder can be difficult to control. I'm sorry that happened to you, Elia. Is that why your leg hurt so much after the accident?"

She nodded. "It stretched the scarring and irritated all of those nerve endings. I tend to have neuralgia in my right foot, anyway, from the burns." She shrugged. "So now you know. I wasn't trying to make it a big secret. It just doesn't usually come up in normal conversation."

"No, I can see that. And really, it's no one's business, anyway."

She stared at him. "I thought that's what you wanted to talk to me about it, so if not that, then what?"

Elia realized she was the one who'd actually assumed that was to be the subject of this conversation and she'd tried to head him off at the pass and, instead, had revealed everything. Only to find out that he wasn't here to grill her about her leg. At all.

He turned a little more to the right so that he faced her directly. "I wanted to talk about what happened at my house."

Her face turned white-hot, and she knew color was pulsing into it at this very minute. Did he know? Had she somehow been louder than she thought she'd been?

"Wh-what do you mean?"

If he knew, she was going to turn in her resignation. No way could she face the man every day knowing that he knew a secret that was much more private than her scars.

Much more horrifying.

"I wanted to apologize for kissing you."

Kissing her? She racked her brain for... Oh! *That* kiss.

Relief swamped her system. Then she laughed. "You want to what? It was on my nose. It wasn't like you—how do you say it?—planted one on me."

His head tilted sideways as if not understanding her reaction at all. "It didn't bother you?"

"Why would it?"

"I don't know, you just seemed to act a little differently after we parted in the parking lot of the bike shop that evening."

Deus do céu. She had. And it had started long before they reached the parking lot. But there was no way she was going to tell him why. That had been a crazy day, and she could only chalk her actions up to shock from the accident combined with feeling vulnerable from how badly her leg hurt. And how sexy he had looked standing there fresh from the shower in bare feet and wet hair. And the tantalizing scent of his soap. And...

"I think maybe it was just shock from the accident."

He blinked like he didn't really believe her. But as long as he didn't challenge her on it, she should be fine. But she definitely didn't want him to think a little kiss on the nose had sent her into some weird head trip where she couldn't look at him straight.

She couldn't. But it had nothing to do with that kiss, which she had thought was sweet, even if she secretly wished it had landed just a little lower.

Seriously, Elia? Haven't you learned your lesson?

Evidently not. But she'd better send herself back through the program and try again. Because she could not go on the way she was now. Especially since she was now conjuring up scenarios where he was asking her to reveal personal facts about herself—like her burns— when nothing could be further from the truth. She'd spewed all of that information out for no reason. No reason at all.

But even so, there was a small part of her that was relieved to have it out in the open. He was the first one at the hospital to really know about it. Despite that, she certainly wasn't going to make it a habit of baring her soul to him. Because that could become a more dangerous prospect. Like wishing he'd kissed her on the mouth?

She shook the question away without answering it. "Well, I'm sure you need to go get ready for surgery. Good luck, even though you won't need it. I was serious when I said you were one of the best in the area. You are, although I'm sure you've been told that many times."

He paused for a long moment. "Yes. But not by you."

The words went right past her before she retrieved them and replayed them, unsure as to whether or not she'd really heard what she thought she'd heard. She had. She just wasn't sure what he meant. But he made it sound like her opinion mattered. That he might have moments of insecurity just like she did. That fact somehow made her smile.

"Well, you have now. So go do what you were born to do."

"Thanks." He gave her a sideways grin. "See you on the other side."

CHAPTER SIX

HE KNEW SHE was there.

Oh, he hadn't looked up to see if she'd actually gone into the viewing room, but he somehow knew she had. That she was watching even as he used his dermatome to remove a section of skin tissue from Matt's clavicle and carefully place it into the collection tray. Hopefully the autograft would take on the first try so he wouldn't have to harvest any more. There was always the chance of failure with a free skin graft, where there was no transfer of a vascular supply to the new location. To help combat that, he was using a split thickness skin graft rather than a full thickness, since it was a little less persnickety about how quickly those vascular highways were constructed.

As the nurse carried the skin away to prep it, he allowed himself to finally glance up. She was there, sitting in the front row. Her eyes met his for a second and she gave him a quick nod.

A spurt of warmth washed through his system. Her approval mattered a little too much, and it bothered him. He shouldn't have even looked up. But what was wrong with needing a little word of encouragement from time to time? There wasn't anything wrong with it. Not inherently. But caring that the encouragement specifically came from Elia should bother him.

He turned his attention back to his patient and did his best to forget she was there. But it wasn't easy. And he didn't like that he was taking even more care than usual with this particular surgery. As if he wanted to impress her.

He didn't. What he wanted was for this young man to have a successful outcome. To go on with his life despite the trauma he'd experienced. It was good that Elia had recommended the teen and his family undergo counseling. It would help them know how to support him without suffocating him or turning overprotective. And it would teach Matt to absorb what had happened to him and maybe even use his trauma for something positive. Like using his story to help another burn victim in the future.

Like what Elia was doing?

Exactly like that. She seemed to have been

able to get past her childhood accident and not only go into nursing in a burn unit, but do more than that. She was helping individual patients like Matt. It was a boon not only for Westlake Memorial as an organization, but also for individual patients. He was sure this wasn't the first time she'd given someone helpful advice. Or supported a fundraising event in a very tangible way.

Maybe instead of apologizing to her, he should be thanking her. But that would involve pulling her aside yet again to talk to her.

And as much as part of him wanted to do exactly that, another part of him wanted to avoid conversing with her more than necessary. Because he was starting to care too much about different aspects of her life. About what she did or didn't do. About what she thought or didn't think...of him.

The nurse came back with the prepped skin, and he used forceps to pick it up and examine it for defects or other problems. He saw none.

"Okay, let's get this done."

With everyone doing their assigned tasks, the graft was attached. Jake had opted to use fine sutures rather than staples, since this was an area that would be highly visible and he didn't want there to be a thick line of scarring where the graft met the rest of the skin of Matt's face.

He rinsed the area to examine it closely and gave himself mental permission to call the surgery a success. "Okay, I think we've gotten what we came for today. Good work, people."

The donor site was covered in a pressure bandage and would heal by second intentions, in which the wound would grow a new layer of skin. So there was no need for suturing that area at all, like they would have needed to do if they'd harvested a full thickness piece.

They woke Matt up, and when he glanced up at him with groggy, confused eyes, Jake gave him a simple thumbs-up sign. "Everything went well. We're going to get you back to your room. Your parents are waiting there to see you."

The teen put his hand up and lightly touched the bandage. And motioned for something. Maybe a mirror.

"You won't be able to see it for several days, and you need to keep your jaw as still as you can to let the new skin attach and form new blood vessels."

He nodded in answer. Jake would reiterate those instructions to his parents, since it was doubtful that Matt would remember much of what was said right now. When he glanced up at the observation window, he noted that Elia was gone. What had he expected, though? That she would stick around to talk to him later?

He patted Matt on the shoulder and then headed out the door to go find the teen's parents. When he got to the room, he was shocked to see that Elia was there, already talking to the parents. He only caught a portion of it, but the part he did was about how good of a job Jake had done.

"Well, thanks for the vote of confidence, but I have a pretty good team around me that helps make that happen."

"Oh, I didn't mean to—"

He gave her a smile that was meant to reassure her that she'd said nothing wrong. "You didn't. I was simply including you as part of that team. The recovery portion is just as important as the actual surgery."

Her face turned pink, something he still found attractive as all get-out. It made him want to see what else would make her blush, before shutting down that line of thought.

Matt's mom smiled. "Any projections as to how visible the scars will be?"

He shot a quick glance at Elia to see what her reaction to that was, since her scars had evidently never healed as smoothly as other people's might have. But she didn't look uncomfortable about the question.

"It won't be so much the scars that are visible as the fact that the skin tone may be slightly different, and there will be no beard growth possible in that area since the hair follicles are different than those in other parts of his jaw. But even that can be altered slightly if he chooses to get hair transplants from other areas of his chin and/or jaw. We can get pretty darn close nowadays."

"Matt will be so happy to hear that. When can we see him?"

"They're just letting him wake up a little more and then he'll come back to the room. Maybe a half hour, tops."

"Thank you again. Will he need more skin graft surgeries?"

"If this one takes the way that I hope it will, he should be good to go as far as skin goes. He'll still need the teeth implants done, but the skin is in place, which is a pretty big thing, since it will help prevent infections from settling into open tissue."

"We are so grateful," his mother said. "So very grateful."

He understood what they meant. Part of it

was probably referring to the surgery itself, but part of it was probably also talking about how lucky they were that Matt's injuries could be treated. That he would be able to live a fairly normal life. Like Elia did. She was pretty damn lucky, too. Some of those deep-tissue injuries required a lot of work to get to them to a place where they could still be functional, even if the tissue didn't look like most people's.

"I'm glad it's turning out the way it is." He glanced at both of them. "Do you have any more questions for me?"

They both shook their heads no. "But we do want to ask Elia a little more about the counseling service she recommended to us."

"Okay, good. You have my cell number. Don't hesitate to give me a call if you have any concerns or questions."

"We will."

Jake turned to go out of the door and heard the next conversation start with, "He was great when I talked to him about my experience, even though my injury happened many years ago."

The door closed behind him, shutting him out of the conversation completely. But that was okay. He'd been fairly anxious to get away from Elia before he ended up having to talk to her alone.

He went to the desk, and before he could help himself, he took the tongs and selected a cookie...bit into it. It tasted as fresh and good as they had a week ago when she'd first started bringing them. Maybe he needed to ask her about getting reimbursed for at least some of the ingredients. The sign-up sheet beside the jar looked new, and when he picked it up, he saw that there was a staple in it and that there were at least three other sheets of paper stapled together. At least a hundred people were now signed up. Just on this floor. He frowned. He didn't think they even had that many patients. Were people from other departments coming over to get cookies? That could get pretty expensive for Elia if she was having to foot the bill for providing refreshments for the whole hospital.

Yes, he was going to have to catch her and see where they stood. He frowned. Wait. Maybe he had an answer for that, one that would help on more than one level. He went into one of the supply cabinets and found a spare glass jar that was used for tongue depressor dispensers. He grabbed a Sharpie and a piece of paper and wrote in big letters:

Cookie Fund. Take a cookie, leave a donation.
That should get the point across. And then

Elia could use the funds to replenish what she'd spent on making all of these.

Except she came out of the room and took one look at the sign and the marker in his hand. "Absolutely not."

"Word has obviously gotten out that there are some pretty good cookies up in the burn unit. I already feel bad that you're having to spend your free time making these. The least that people can do is donate something to the cause." With that, he took out five dollars and dropped it into the jar.

"My mom is actually bringing more cookies up tomorrow. So it's not just me making them."

"Well, then you can give her some of the money, as well. There won't be a lot, I'm sure, but maybe it will at least buy some of the ingredients."

She shook her head but smiled. "Oh, you don't know my mom. She does it because she loves it. And she makes decent money as a pastry chef in the Austin area. People come from miles around to sample what she makes."

This time, though, she didn't say anything about the bread she'd promised her mom would make for them. And he wasn't about to bring it up.

At that moment, the service elevator pinged

and the doors opened. Matt's bed was being wheeled toward his hospital room. One of the orderlies was smiling at something the teen evidently said—despite the fact that Jake had just warned the kid to move his lower jaw as little as possible. It had already been immobilized due to the transplanted bone, but even using the muscles of his lips to form words would jar the skin grafts. He started to go over there, only to have Elia place her hand over his arm.

He looked at her in question.

"His parents will remind him. He doesn't need both you and them getting on to him." Her eyes were gentle. "He is still groggy from the anesthesia. Believe me, if anyone wants this graft to take, it's Matt. He won't purposely do anything to sabotage that."

He relaxed. "I guess you're right. I can be a little overbearing at times."

"Who, you?" Although her eyes were wide and innocent, there was laughter behind them that told him she was joking.

"Very funny. You've never gotten on to a patient for doing something that could be detrimental to their health?"

"Yes, of course, if they were willfully flouting doctor's recommendations. But not right after surgery, when people's thought processes can be affected by the anesthesia meds. It does contain an amnesiac."

"I'm quite aware of that. But point taken. If I see him doing a lot of talking tomorrow, though, I can't promise I won't say something to him."

"If he's still doing it tomorrow, then I'll beat you to it. But I doubt that he will be."

"I'll hold you to that, Elia."

She blinked for a second before sucking down a deep breath and leaning her hip against the nurse's desk. "How is Randy? Have you heard anything else?"

"No, but I plan on calling him sometime later today. I know he's home and was doing well as of yesterday."

"Good. Have you done any more training for the festival?"

"No. And the bike group isn't getting together this week in deference to Randy. People chipped in to get him a new ride, since his bike was totaled." Someone had asked him to mention it to Elia, but she'd only been with them once, so he hadn't felt right asking her to contribute.

She opened the jar and took out the five-dollar bill and then went behind the counter to pull out a wallet. Probably hers. She extracted a twenty and handed him both bills. "Can you add this to what everyone contributed?"

"Elia…"

"I want to. I'm happy to be able to at least do something for him."

She pulled his hand toward her and placed the money on his palm and then closed his fingers around it. Her touch was warm and sure, and he wished it had lasted a little longer than it had. "I'll give it to the bike shop. They'll know what to do with it. Maybe they can start a fund to get him a new helmet or other piece of equipment to go with the bike, which has already been bought."

"How long before he can ride again?"

"I would assume at least five more weeks or however long it takes for his elbow to heal."

She frowned. "He was planning on participating in the bike festival next weekend, wasn't he?"

"He was, but there's no way he'll be able to."

"I get it. But it still makes me sad for him."

Sheryll came out of a room and moved toward them. That was Jake's signal to move on, since she'd kind of given them a funny look when they'd gone off together earlier today.

The last thing he needed was for a rumor about them to start making its way around the hospital.

"I need to get back to work, and I assume you do, too."

She grinned. "Nope. I'm off as of an hour and a half ago. I just wanted to watch Matt's surgery, so I stuck around."

"I'm sure he appreciated that."

Sheryll glanced at them as she arrived at the desk. "Who appreciated what?"

At least this was a question he could answer without making anyone uncomfortable.

"We were talking about Matt's surgery and the fact that Elia stayed to watch it."

"I was wondering why you were still on the floor." The other nurse glanced at her watch. "Did your mom make it in?"

"That's tomorrow."

"Oh, that's right. It's been a crazy day. But mine is about to end, too, and then I'm taking a long weekend off."

Jake did remember hearing something about that, whether it was an overheard conversation or whether she'd said it when Elia had mentioned going to watch the surgery. He smiled at her and said, "Well, I hope you have a wonderful weekend."

"Thanks. I'm sure we will. It's been a while since my husband and I have gotten away together."

"Enjoy," said Elia. "And I'm going to take off, too. See you on Monday, Sheryll, and I'll see you…?"

"I'm working tomorrow," Jake said. "You?"

"Same. So I guess I'll see you tomorrow."

Was it his imagination or did she not look very happy about the fact that they would be working with each other the next day? Well, it couldn't be helped, so she'd better get used to it, otherwise they were both going to have a big problem. Like the fact that he was finding himself worrying about things like those damned cookies and how much time, energy and money she was spending on the bike festival, when promoting it was something he should be doing.

"See you then."

With that, Jake turned and headed back to his office, leaving the two of them to talk about whatever they wanted to.

And if it was about him?

He couldn't imagine anything they might have to say about him. And really, he didn't care. Or at least he shouldn't. That didn't mean that part of him didn't wonder, though. But as long as they weren't making plans to match him up with anyone, he wasn't going to worry about it. Just to be sure, he went to his office and dug down to the bottom of one of his desk drawers. He pulled out last year's copy of *Daily Gossip* and stared at the headline for a minute. There was a huge picture of Samantha on the cover with a distressed look on her face. Above it were the words Plastic Surgeon Abandons Model on French Riviera. A second, smaller photo was of him with an angry look on his face, but the anger wasn't directed at Sam. It was at the photographers who'd always dogged their every step back when they'd been an item.

He'd met Sam while at a conference in Dallas, where she had a second home. They'd hit it off and had started seeing each other. They'd been able to keep their relationship a secret for a while at his request, but once it got out, the press had a field day with it and speculated whether or not she'd been one of his patients. Then, when things went sour, there was the tabloid article along with her angry social media post, and even more speculation had happened. So much so that his hospital asked some hard questions that he'd answered truthfully. Things had blown over, but it had been a cautionary tale about rumors and gossip. One he wasn't likely to forget. So when Sheryll had looked at him and Elia with speculation in her eyes, he'd been only too happy to leave the scene, before that speculation grew into something else. He could only hope that Elia wasn't the type to fuel those kinds of rumors, although he didn't get that vibe from her.

But the less the head nurse saw them doing things together, the better. So he would make it a point to treat Elia just like any other nurse. Because that's what she was, right? She was nothing special to him.

A quick twinge in his midsection made him wonder if that was absolutely the truth. But even if it wasn't, he was somehow going to need to get back to a place where it would become the truth. No matter how hard that might prove to be. It was either that or face the possibility of something like this—he tossed the paper to the side of his desk—happening all over again.

Sheryll leaned closer. "Is there something I should know?"

"Know?" Elia tilted her head and looked at the other woman.

"You guys have been hanging out a little bit,

haven't you? First the group bike ride and now Matt's surgery?"

She frowned. "Uh, that wasn't exactly hanging out. We were in two separate rooms, for one thing. And *Matt* asked me to stay, and I did as a favor to him…the patient, not Jake."

"Okay, I get that."

"And he was here at the desk because he had the dumb idea that he should take up donations for the cookies I've been making."

Sheryll nodded. "I think that's a great idea. There have been a lot of people eating them, Elia. It has to be costing a fortune."

"No, it's not. Besides, I really like baking and haven't had the chance to do as much of it as I used to. Before I became a nurse. And now, I'm too exhausted by the time I get home."

Sheryll nodded. "The job does take such a lot of emotional energy out of you. I'm the same way when I get home in the evenings. I don't have much motivation to do much of anything. So I don't know how you can bake cookies. It's like you're still working for Westlake even in your off hours, since it is their event."

"I guess I don't see it that way. I'm doing something besides nursing, so that has to count for something, right?"

"I guess. But I am still going to leave this

donation jar up. Because I think it's the right thing to do."

Elia rolled her eyes and said, "Fine. Do whatever you want to do."

"Believe me, I will, so leave this here."

"Fine." She pretended to flounce off in a huff but knew her friend would see right through her. In reality, though, her and Jake's concern warmed her heart and made her feel like she'd made the right decision when she'd moved to Dallas to take this job. It felt right. And right now that was the only thing she was going to dwell on.

CHAPTER SEVEN

ELIA'S MOM SWEPT into the hospital with all of the subtlety of a freight train, and it made her cringe, even though she knew her parents meant well. She'd already been scheduled to work, and she'd asked them to make themselves at home in her small apartment, but of course her mom had wanted to see where her new job was and must have had her dad drive her over to Westlake Memorial.

It was understandable, but she also knew that Jake was somewhere on the floor, and for some reason she didn't want her mom meeting him. She was always going on about how Elia should meet some nice guy and settle down. She'd met plenty of nice guys. They just never seemed to want long-term relationships. More like the friends-with-benefits type of agreements, and she was no longer interested in doing that. Because she got emotionally attached, even when the man in question didn't seem to. She'd asked a friend if there was something she was doing...if she was too clingy, too needy, and they said no. That the men were jerks. But apart from the guy who'd pulled the covers up over them, could they really *all* be jerks? Or was she just attracted to shallow, jerkish types?

Regardless, the last thing she wanted was for her mom to swoop in and start taking notes on the men at the hospital and ask embarrassing questions. Questions that she wasn't about to answer. Not that she knew too many of the men yet...besides Jake. And she didn't even really know him, right?

Except he'd been willing to save her life on the bike ride that day. And she'd fantasized about him in his bathtub afterward.

Oh, Lord. She definitely didn't want her mom meeting him.

Her mom gave her a big hug and motioned for her dad to put the three boxes he was carrying on the desk. *"Biscoitos."* She looked at the jar holding the current batch and added, "It looks like they are just in time, too. Are you sure you don't want something other than bicycles on some of them? Maybe some with just flowers?"

Her mom spoke in Portuguese, even though

her English was really good. It used to embarrass her when she did that in public, but she'd come to understand that it was her mom's heart language and that it made the conversation more intimate to speak to her daughter in "their" language. Her dad, however, had long switched over. So Elia had learned to talk to them in two different languages.

She laughed. "It's for the bike festival, Mom, so no, I don't think flowers or ballerinas or fairies would get that message across."

"Just asking. Hopefully next year the fundraiser will be something different. Something more...interesting."

"They've been doing this for quite a few years and it's successful, so I don't think they're going to change it anytime soon."

Her dad patted her arm and leaned over to kiss her on the cheek. "Don't let her fool you. She's been trying to make every cookie different and has been looking up countless ideas on that Pinterest site."

The thought of her mom scrolling through endless pictures on social media made her laugh again. Especially when she swatted her husband's arm. "I have not. I do have an imagination, you know."

"Whatever you say, dear." Her dad did respond to his wife in Portuguese.

Time to send them both on their way before they got into one of their little heated discussions about this or that and someone came along. It was all in love, but sometimes it sure didn't sound that way.

"I gave you the keys to the apartment. Why don't you guys get some lunch and then head over there. I should be home in an hour or two." She still needed to check Matt's bandages and make sure the graft was doing okay, and she had a few other patients she needed to see.

Just then the elevator doors opened, and when she saw who got off, she closed her eyes for a second and sent up a silent prayer. Great. Just what she needed, although it was inevitable that they would meet. She'd just rather it happen later rather than sooner and on Elia's terms.

He spotted her, and of course he came over to get updates on some of the patients. She tried to edge away from the desk, but her mom's eyes followed her every move. "Hi, Dr. Callin, I was just getting ready to check on Matt."

Jake's head tilted. "It hasn't been Dr. Callin in a while. Is something wrong?"

"And who is this, *filhinha*?"

The plastic surgeon's eyes changed as soon as he heard her mother speak and gave her an apologetic look. He definitely understood now. Now that it was too late.

"This is Dr. Jakob Callin. He's head of Westlake's burn unit. Jake, this is my mom and dad."

Her mother stood on tiptoe and kissed his cheek in Portuguese fashion, which made Elia wince. Jake didn't seem shocked by it, though. He just smiled at her.

"Tersia and Nelson. Nice to meet you." She glanced at her daughter. "Of course Elia hasn't mentioned anyone from her work yet, and we've been very curious."

Oh, Mom, please don't do this. Not with Jake, of all people.

"She's very good at her job," Jake said. "And of course we're so grateful to you and Elia for providing cookies to advertise the fundraiser. They've been very popular. She also mentioned you make wonderful bread."

He sent a glint Elia's way, and she crinkled her nose, instinctively knowing that he was teasing her. But he had no idea what he was about to unleash. No idea at all. She started a mental countdown and waited for it.

"Yes, I do. You must come over to Elia's apartment tomorrow. I will fix you a traditional Portuguese meal, although the bread won't be as good without my bread oven."

And there it was. Just like she knew it would be.

"Oh, I didn't mean for you to..." Jake sounded startled by the invitation.

This time it was Elia who sent him a raised brow. He'd asked for it. And now there was nothing she could do about it. It would be up to him to say he had other plans, which she hoped to hell that he would. For both their sakes.

"But I insist. If you have no plans." Her mom pushed forward with the invitation.

Evidently her father was not going to step in and intervene, which was probably for the best, because it might make her mom dig in her heels even further.

"I don't. If Elia is okay with me coming over, that is."

"But of course she is. Aren't you, *filha*?" Her mom was now looking at her as if surprised that Jake would even think that might be the case.

"Of course I am." Her delivery was a little

wooden, but there was no way she was going to act overjoyed. She really didn't want him *or* her mom getting the wrong idea.

"Let me know the time, then, and I'll see that I'm there. But please don't go to a lot of work."

He obviously didn't know her mom. Or their culture. Of course she would go to a lot of work. She loved to entertain. It was ingrained in her ancestral DNA.

"I won't," her mom said. "How about seven in the evening? That is about the time we normally eat."

"Seven is perfect. I'll see you there."

Her mom's eyes widened. "So you know where my daughter lives?"

"No, but I was going to have her text me the address." This time, his response was a little more cautious, as if finally realizing what could happen if he wasn't careful.

"I see. Okay, well, we'll let you both get back to…work. And we'll see you tomorrow."

"Thanks again for the invitation."

Her parents headed for the elevator and got on, her mom waving all the way up until the doors swallowed them from view.

Elia plopped onto one of the tall stools and looked at him. "I am so sorry, Jake. You don't have to go. I can tell her you realized you have another commitment."

"Do you not want me to come?"

Was that a trick question? Why would he even want to? "It's not that. I just don't want you to feel bamboozled into a dinner you don't want."

"I haven't heard that term in a while." He smiled. "And I have to say, 'bamboozled' sounds so much more sophisticated when said with your accent."

Her face heated, but this time it was a good warmth. One that was a whole lot better than the embarrassment that she'd felt over her mom's antics. But that was common with her mother, who seemed to know just how to maneuver people to do what she wanted them to do. And she'd done an expert job with Jake. She'd gotten him to do exactly what she wanted. And the only thing was, Elia was a little afraid that dinner might not be the end of it. So she needed to at least put their relationship at the hospital back on professional footing. To do that, she decided to act as if that invitation to dinner had never happened.

So when he suggested they go and see Matt together, she jumped at it. "I was actually just going in to see how his graft was doing."

"And I was actually headed there when I got off that elevator a few moments ago." He motioned for her to precede him. "Shall we?"

Probably accepting that dinner invitation hadn't been one of Jake's smartest moves, but it had been so unexpected that he hadn't been able to think quickly enough to get out of it. Then again, he was the one who'd brought it on himself by mentioning homemade bread.

And hell, if the word "bamboozled" hadn't been the sexiest thing Jake had ever heard. It sent heat spiraling through him and made him think he wouldn't have minded being bamboozled by Elia in any number of ways.

By the time they got into Matt's room, though, he'd regained his senses and was able to concentrate on the teen. His parents were there, as they'd been every step of this journey. He shook their hands. Gracie was nowhere to be seen, but it was likely that she was working somewhere over the summer. They did a quick check of the pressure bandage covering the site and it was intact. "You're being careful to not move your jaw much, right?"

The teen nodded and wrote something on a whiteboard. "Not talking more than necessary."

Jake nodded. "And you understand why that's so important. Movement of the graft is not your friend right now. The tissue needs to make its own vascular field to grow and thrive—and those new blood vessels are extremely fragile in the beginning."

Matt moved his closed fist up and down in what Jake recognized as the signed word for yes. Then he wrote, "How long before the bandage comes off?"

"About eight days, although it's not going to look perfect when it comes off. The final result will take time and patience."

The teen's face didn't change and Jake wasn't sure what he was thinking. But he didn't want to lie and then take the bandages off and have Matt have a meltdown.

Veronica spoke up for the first time. "Matt also wanted to know how long he'll need to stay in the hospital."

That was also a common question. One with a complicated answer. "We're looking at about two weeks to make sure the graft and the donor site both heal well, especially since we'll be dealing with other surgeries. Your tooth implants won't be able to be done until your jaw and your skin graft are both healed enough."

This time Matt did frown, and Elia, who'd

been scurrying around getting vitals and checking supplies, stopped what she was doing and moved back to the bed, putting her hand on the teen's arm. "I know it seems like a long time, and I was impatient, too, when I had my surgeries, but if you rush it and things don't look the way you'd hoped they would, you'll always wonder if it was something you did or simply the way your body heals."

Was that what she'd done? Tried to rush her healing process and then wondered if that was why she had contractures or why her body developed keloids? She acted like she knew it was her body's genetic makeup that was at fault, but was there something more going on below the surface?

Matt seemed to relax into the pillows with a slight nod. Elia pulled Veronica to the side and said something to her, to which the teen's mom gripped both her hands before giving her a long hug.

Elia was good at empathizing. He'd never had anyone complain about his bedside manner, but he also knew himself well enough to know that he tended to be more matter-of-fact and wasn't wired to say things that met people's emotional needs.

It was one of Samantha's complaints about

him. Although she'd had a long laundry list of
faults that she supposedly hadn't been able to
deal with. That along with the request she'd
made at the very end of their relationship had
done them in as a couple. She'd been really un-
happy about his refusal, although she hadn't
wanted to talk about it later. But Sam had also
had "people" who specialized in smoothing
the way for her. The funny thing was, it was
one of her staff members who'd communi-
cated with him while she was in France on a
job that, while Sam would "always love him
and cherish the time they'd spent together," she
wanted to break things off. She hadn't even
had the nerve to tell him herself. And though
he'd been more relieved than angry, almost
immediately afterward those tabloids had exploded with the news that he'd abandoned her
while they'd been on holiday. It was almost
as if she'd planned things right down to the
headline.

A few weeks later, she was dating an actor.
Someone much better suited to her. He was
happy for her. And extremely happy for himself. He understood they had a child now.

He didn't want to go through that again.
Ever. Did he think he might find someone he'd
want to settle down with? He didn't see it hap-

pening anytime soon. He was happy with his life the way it was.

Glancing at Elia, he saw she was watching him, and he realized he'd been lost in his own world for several minutes. So he shook off his thoughts and went over to where she was still standing. In a low voice, she said, "Would it be okay if I contacted the counseling center to see if they could do their first couple of sessions here in Matt's hospital room? I really think he could benefit from it."

"I think that's a great idea." He had been worried a little over Matt's demeanor. It was hard to be a teenager with a girlfriend and have to not talk or move more than necessary. Who had to sit in a hospital room for more than two weeks while the world went on without him. "Is Gracie still in the picture?" He kept his voice as low as Elia's had been.

"She is. She's been really great. But I can tell Matt is worried about how long she'll stick around. I remember being that age and scared that anything I did would make people look at me weird. I think the thing he's worried most about is being disfigured for life. That he'll look like a monster or something. For someone who's always been popular, it's a hard blow."

Out of the corner of his eye, he saw Elia shift

her weight onto her bad leg. Had she been worried about that, even though her burns had not been in a visible place? Just then Matt started waving his arms at them and held up his whiteboard. "What are you guys talking about?" it read.

They moved back over to the bed and Elia spoke up. "Would you like to start meeting with your counselor here at the hospital, since you'll be here a little longer because of your grafts? You could ask Gracie if she wants to join you, if that's something you'd be interested in."

He nodded emphatically and scribbled on his board. "Would they do that? Meet here?"

"I can go call them right after I leave here. If Dr. Callin writes up an order for it, it's more likely to be covered by insurance."

All eyes in the room shifted to him. There was a fine balance in his line of work to order treatments that were necessary while not incurring unnecessary costs to the patient or insurance companies. But he did think if the center that Elia had talked to would consider coming to the hospital, then that would be a good thing. A necessary thing. "I'll be happy to write it up as necessary, if it helps with insurance coverage."

Matt erased what was on his board and simply wrote, "Thank you."

He nodded. "Thank Elia. She's the one who thought of it."

Just then one of the nurses stuck her head in. "You're needed in the ER, Dr. Callin."

Elia turned to Matt and said, "I'll call the counseling center and let you know when they can come."

Not *if* they could come. But when. He had never seen her truly angry, but he knew from experience on that first day that she would move heaven and earth to see that her patients got what they needed.

She left the room when he did and waited as Brittany filled them in. "The squad just brought in a three-year-old who pulled a pot of boiling water onto herself. Scald burns down the front of her."

"Headed that way." He turned to Elia. "Let me know how that call goes."

"I will. Let me know how the child is."

He nodded. "Will do."

Some medical staff had adopted a thick skin—a kind of defense mechanism—to deal with the traumas that came into hospitals day in and day out. To have a tender heart was to be in danger of burning out emotionally.

So he'd been surprised by Elia's request to let her know how the kid was, especially since she'd been injured as a child herself. Brittany walked away to do other things, and Jake found himself touching Elia's hand. "Are you okay?"

She didn't ask what he was talking about, just looked him in the eye. "Little kids are always harder, for some reason."

Gripping her fingers, he gently squeezed. "I'll let you know. Promise."

"Thanks, Jake. Really."

"Not a problem." Then he let go of her and headed toward the elevator and whatever awaited him on the ground floor.

Elia didn't have to wait a super long time before learning how Jake's little patient was doing. She'd been able to call the counseling center, who promised someone would be out tomorrow morning, despite it being Sunday. She'd sagged in relief. All it would take was for Matt to reach rock bottom and impulsively do something that would damage everything Jake had worked so hard to do for the teen and his family.

The service elevator opened, and the first thing she heard was a child crying, even as the plastic surgeon exited the car and waited while two hospital staff members wheeled the bed into the room. Elia hurried over to them. The little girl seemed so tiny on the huge hospital bed. Her heart cramped. "Let's put her in Room Four for now."

She pushed through the door first, mentally taking stock of the supplies in the room that Jake might need. Once they got to the room, Jake actually slid his hands beneath the girl's back, carefully avoiding the front. Elia could see angry red skin already beginning to blister across the tiny girl's chest and legs, where the clothing had been cut away.

Second-degree burns at least. And probably areas where the damage went deeper. The girl screamed louder when Jake moved her over to the bed in the room, even though he was being extremely gentle. "Her parents?"

He glanced at her. "They're talking to social workers and the police right now, but they'll be up in a few minutes."

"*Deus*. It wasn't on purpose, was it?"

"No. From all accounts, they had company and the mom was fixing a large lunch and went to talk to her guests while pasta water was heating up." He pulled in a visible breath, stroking the child's face, which thankfully looked devoid of burns. "Carly evidently pulled a little stool over that she used to help her mom do the dishes and they heard scream- ing and found the pot on the floor and the tod- dler covered with water. They did the right thing and put her under a cold shower, but her clothes held the heat against her skin until they got her cooled off."

"And the police?"

"It's routine to ask questions whenever a child has scalds like this, but they are pretty distraught."

She could imagine. Snatches of her own mom's face as she'd held her in her arms after she was burned were etched in her memory. The fear. The horror. The self-condemnation for not noticing that Elia was getting so close to the fire.

She moved over to the girl. She bent over to talk soothingly to her before remembering that she'd seen a Binky on the gurney she'd been brought in on. "Wait here with her for a minute."

She went outside, glad to find that the order- lies were still waiting for the elevator to arrive on the floor. Just then the doors opened. "Can you hold that for a minute?"

Quickly walking over to them, she glanced at the bed and didn't see anything for a second.

Then she lifted the pillow and found a pink pacifier. She normally wouldn't have given it to the child without permission, but right now she'd do anything she could to comfort the little girl.

She returned to the room, and when she offered it to the crying toddler, she opened her mouth and took it. Her little lashes were wet with tears, and Elia couldn't imagine how much pain she was in. Burn injuries hurt. A lot. And for a child who didn't understand what was going on...

"Good thinking. I just got a text that her parents are on their way up," Jake said.

"Okay. What do you want me to do first?" Was he asking her to intercept the parents so he could finish assessing the child?

"Let's get an IV started."

Starting an IV on a child who was in pain or scared was always a tricky process. But fortunately her parents came into the room and were there for the procedure, soothing Carly and holding her arm while Elia placed the catheter. In less than thirty seconds it was in and taped in place. Fortunately that hand was free of burns. Then they were in treatment mode, assessing which of the burns were the deepest and needed immediate attention. It was then that they were able to give some meds for pain. Once that was done, Carly was much less agitated and was able to sleep through some of the procedures, while her mom sat next to the bed and stroked her head, silent tears streaming down her face.

Elia had treated plenty of children since she'd gone through her specialty training, but it was still hard to see them in pain. Especially when the wounds needed to be debrided.

As if reading her mind, Jake pulled the parents aside while Carly slept. "The burns are serious, don't get me wrong, but from what I can see the worst of them are second-degree rather than third."

"Does that mean no scarring?" her mom asked.

"The deeper ones still can in some instances, but we'll work hard to give her the best outcome possible. If the area was small, we could probably send her home with some care instructions, but because this affects a large area of her torso, we want to keep her for a bit. She already has blistering, which will spread, and in some places individual blisters will join together and she'll lose the top layer of skin. What's underneath will be raw and very tender. That's when the danger of infection sets in."

Carly's dad had been really quiet but finally spoke up. "Do what you need to do. One of us will be here around the clock, if possible."

"I think that can be arranged. The recliner next to the bed folds flat, but we'll want to limit visitors to her room, just to reduce the chance of microbes being brought into her room."

"How long before she'll be released?"

"Give us a couple of days to make that decision. It depends on what her skin does or doesn't do."

"We have three other children. Carly is our youngest. Can they see her? They're all scared and upset. My mom is with them right now."

Elia ached for them. Even though the other kids needed the reassurance that Carly would be okay, Jake was absolutely right that the chance of infection would start soon. As soon as her skin began peeling to reveal the deeper layers, the danger of that happening increased.

"We can set something up like a Zoom meeting or a virtual hospital visit like they did during the pandemic. But we really don't want any more people in here than necessary."

Carly whimpered in her sleep and her mom immediately went over to try to console her. She lifted her hand, as if trying to figure out where she could touch and where she couldn't. Elia leaned down. "Just stroke her forehead and talk to her. She just wants to know that someone she loves is here."

As Carly's mom did her best to reassure her child, Elia slid from the room to try to give her some privacy. Jake had evidently stepped outside to talk to Carly's dad. It was probably for the best, since as soon as he walked back into that room, it would be to start treating her burns. All she could pray was that, since Carly was young and healthy, she would heal quickly and she would experience as little pain as possible.

Wasn't that what every human being wanted? To experience as little pain as possible? Yes. And it was a good reminder that pain wasn't always physical. It was sometimes emotional. And that pain might not leave physical scars, but she knew from experience that it could leave invisible wounds that lasted long after the causative agent was removed. Like being with someone who didn't want to look at your scars while making love to you.

Heading over to the nurses' desk, she worked on updating their patient information. And in doing so, she tried to forget that tiny touch to the hand that Jake had given her earlier. Because it had been sweet and warming and far too welcome. She was starting to like his presence too much, and for Elia, that could be a very dangerous proposition. One she would do well to avoid, unless she was willing to risk being hurt. Again.

CHAPTER EIGHT

JAKE CLUTCHED THE bottle of red wine that he'd brought as a thank-you for Tersia and Nelson. He'd thrown his bike onto the carrier on the back of his SUV just in case. In case of what? It wasn't likely that Elia was going to want to leave her mom and dad in order to go bike riding with him. He wasn't sure what had possessed him to do it. But with the bike festival next week, he needed to get some training time in while he could. If worse came to worst, he could leave the bike on the back of his vehicle and take a ride during his lunch hour tomorrow or something.

Knocking on the door, he was surprised when less than fifteen seconds went by before someone opened it. It was Elia. She motioned him inside.

"I brought this for your mom and dad for inviting me. But since it's your house, I'm not sure who I should give it to."

"My parents. They'll appreciate the gesture. Wine is actually a customary hostess gift in Portugal. And since she's made a traditional pork dish, it'll pair perfectly with it."

She smiled, and he couldn't hold back his own grin. It felt homey and comfortable to be standing here talking with her like this. Like he really was meeting her parents for the first time.

Except this wasn't that kind of occasion at all.

"Good to know, since I guessed."

"You guessed correctly." She again motioned him inside. "Come in, please."

Her apartment was just as comfortable as their conversation had been, and he could definitely see the Portuguese influence here. Clay plates with blue and white glaze were hung on the walls in the dining room. Almost every free surface had some sort of representation of Portuguese pottery. It was beautiful and fit who Elia was to a tee.

Despite the heat of the day, she still wasn't wearing shorts or even a sundress. Instead she was dressed in a long, loose skirt that looked both comfortable and safe as far as her leg went. He still hadn't seen the scars, but for there to be contractures the damage had to be pretty rough.

And he wasn't likely to see them, although the surgeon in him wondered if there was anything that could still be done to ease the pull. He'd dissected various surgical procedures in his head, knowing that he would never suggest them. It was Elia's body and her choice as far as what she allowed to be done to it.

It was unlikely even if he did offer to examine her that she would go through with surgery. She'd lived with her leg like it was for a long time. She was comfortable with how it functioned and he needed to let her be.

At that moment, Tersia came out of the kitchen with Nelson following close behind.

"Ah, Jakob. It's so good for you to come." Elia's mom's accent was much more pronounced than that of her daughter, and she gave more weight to the last syllable of his name than she had the first. He wondered if Elia would do the same. He thought she might have said his full name before but couldn't remember. He had to admit he loved to hear the nurse talk. Her words rolled through his senses like fine scotch, and he sometimes found himself paying more attention to her cadence than the phrases themselves. Although if he concentrated hard enough…

Which he did. Because he didn't want to embarrass himself by having to ask her to repeat herself. Although it was damned tempting at times.

Cut it out, Callin.

He would assume Tersia and Elia spoke Portuguese when in each other's company, and so while Elia worked in an English-speaking job, there wouldn't be as much need for Tersia to speak the language. Except, hadn't Elia told him that she worked in a bakery, cooking traditional pastries? Yes, but they also probably had a good-sized Portuguese or Brazilian clientele, if that's what their business catered to.

"*Mãe*, Jake brought wine for dinner."

Okay, even without saying his whole name, it had still come out warm and slightly accented. And having his name whispered against his skin in the heat of passion…how would it sound then?

He shut off those thoughts in a hurry, when he realized both women were now looking at him. "I'm sorry, did you say something?"

"I simply said thank you, Jakob." Tersia's expression was a little sharper than it had been, and her eyes were scouring across his face as if searching for something.

Something she wouldn't find, if he had his way. The last thing he wanted was for some woman's mother to try to play matchmaker. Not that that's what she'd been doing. He knew he was acting kind of strange and that's probably why she'd looked at him sideways. He'd better get his head on straight or there would be a lot more than sideways glances. She'd be asking some hard questions. Ones he really didn't want to answer.

Just then Nelson came in and walked over to give his hand a firm clasp. "Good to see you again. Sorry I was late getting to the door. Tersia had me in the kitchen waiting on the bread to finish cooking. I think you'll like it."

Nelson's speech was reminiscent of Elia's. His English, like hers, was excellent, but there remained a tiny bit of an accent. Enough of one to give their way of speaking an exotic flavor that made you want to sit and listen to them.

"I'm sure I'll like all of it, if that wonderful aroma is anything to go by."

"You must come in and sit, while I uncork the wine. Dinner is almost ready." Elia's mom led the way into the living room as if the space were hers rather than her daughter's. Elia threw him a pained smile and mouthed "sorry."

He shook his head and touched her arm as a way of telling her not to worry about it. Her answering smile was much more at ease. "Why don't you sit on the couch and I'll help Mom with whatever else needs to be done. I hope you're hungry. She always makes enough for an army. Seriously. You don't have twenty friends joining us, do you?"

"Sorry, no." He chuckled and everything seemed okay again. He liked being able to joke about things with her in a way he rarely did with other colleagues. There just wasn't much time or the opportunity, since so much revolved around their work.

Well, tonight didn't involve work, and he might as well just settle in and enjoy that fact. He might even be able to unwind. Really unwind. Something he'd wondered if he'd even be able to do when he'd left his apartment an hour ago. Maybe he could after all.

Suddenly, he was looking forward to spending time with them and getting to know Elia and her folks a little better. It was rare that he enjoyed a meal with friends or anyone else, so he would just sit back and allow himself to eat and laugh and give himself permission not to dwell on work or the cases he was currently working on. Those would all still be there tomorrow. And so would he.

The pork with clams in its rich, flavorful sauce proved to be every bit as good as Nelson had said it would be. Even better, actually. And he was enjoying the stories of Elia and her brother when they were kids.

"And then Elia lifted up her hand to throw the seeds toward the pigeons, but they decided she was being too slow about it and one landed right on top of her head. On top of the cute little white beret she had insisted on wearing to the National Bird Park. And that beret..." Tersia smothered a laugh with the back of her hand. "That *puro branco* beret—soon wasn't pure white anymore. And what the bird had dripped down onto her nose." She clapped her hands. "If you could have seen Eliana's expression..."

Jake could picture the pure look of surprise that must have been on a young Elia's face. He laughed again, as he'd been doing for the last half hour.

She chuckled. "I did not invite that pigeon to use me as a perch, nor did I invite it to..."

She swirled her hand in the air to get the point across.

"And what did you do once it did both of those things?"

She leaned her shoulder in to bump against his. "Well, I can tell you what I didn't do. I didn't wear that beret ever again. I'm not sure what even happened to it."

"Oh, I still have it," Tersia said. "It's been professionally cleaned, but it holds a special memory. Her grandmother made it for her."

Elia's eyes widened. "She did? I didn't remember that. I feel badly about never wearing it again, then."

Tersia came over and kissed her on the cheek. "I had enough pictures of you in it that day to make her think it was your favorite garment. I certainly never told her about what the bird did to it. She might have burned the thing until it was nothing but ashes."

As soon as the words came out, her mom stopped talking and covered her mouth with her palm, a look of horror crossing her face. Then she wrapped her arms around her daughter's shoulders. "Forgive me. That did not come out the way I intended it to."

"*Mamãe*, it is fine. You don't need to worry every time you mention something burning."

Tersia didn't look convinced. If anything, her distress seemed to grow. "If only I hadn't been paying as much attention to Tomás that day."

Elia gave him a helpless look, as if this subject had been repeated ad infinitum. "So was I, *Mãe*. So was I. You were not to blame."

Tomás must be a relative. Or a close friend.

As if she felt like he needed an explanation, Tersia said, "Elia was burned as a child while helping her brother learn how to walk. She backed into a fire and fell on it."

He nodded, understanding that Elia was feeling pretty uncomfortable about this subject appearing on the radar. "She told me about her accident. And although I know it was hard for all of you to go through, it has given Elia a wonderful way of empathizing with her patients, something she might not be able to do if she didn't intimately understand what it felt like to go through all of the pain and treatments that our patients have to endure."

Nelson, who was still sitting at the table, tossed him a grateful look. "I've said this very thing to Elia, and she agrees that it helps her do her job, don't you, *filha*?"

"Yes. Absolutely. I love my job. And it does help me understand them, even though no one has had the exact same experience that I had." Under the table, her knee touched his as if thanking him for saying what he had. Or maybe she'd just accidentally touched him and it meant nothing at all. Except, she didn't remove the pressure like she might have otherwise, so he nudged her back.

And when she turned toward him and smiled...

He was transfixed, unable to move for several seconds before finally shaking himself free and including the rest of her family in his return smile. He shared a little about Matt without revealing his name or any identifying information and said what a help Elia had been the first time he actually met her.

"You actually met me before that. You just don't remember."

Tersia murmured, "But you remember her now, don't you."

There was something about the way she said the words that made her daughter say, *"Mamãe..."* as if her mom had said something wrong.

But she hadn't. Elia was pretty damned memorable. "I do, for sure."

She threw a look at Jake. And he couldn't for the life of him understand what it meant.

But all she said was, "Mom, are we ready for dessert?"

"We are. I hope you like," she said to Jake. "We call them *filhós de abobora*. At the bakery, we call them fried pumpkin cakes, but they're not like your traditional American cake. They are Elia's favorite thing. I'll go get them."

There was something about trying something that was Elia's "favorite" that made him anticipate whatever this dessert was that much more.

When Tersia brought in a plate of what looked like misshapen donut holes, he was immediately intrigued. These were golden brown and sprinkled with sugar. And the smell was wonderful.

"Cinnamon?"

"Yes," Tersia said. "They do have cinnamon and sugar sprinkled on them, and I mix a little cinnamon in with the pumpkin. At Christmas time, *filhoses* are sometimes made with decorative iron molds that are heated in hot oil, dipped into a pumpkin batter and then plunged back in the oil to fry until they come free of the mold."

"They are *sooo* good." The way Elia drew out the word made him take a quick breath.

Anything that got that kind of reaction out of her had to be heaven on earth. And damn if it didn't have him salivating for the dessert. But it wasn't just that. He wanted her. To feed her those desserts and hear her make little sounds as she savored them.

Jake swallowed, suddenly feeling like he was in over his head and wanting things he damned well shouldn't want. And yet he did.

Elia's mom set the tray of pumpkin cakes on the table and then went over to a small sideboard and picked up some blue and white dessert plates that matched the set they had used for dinner. They kind of reminded him of the Wedgwood dinnerware they had in the States, but these were heavier, with a more pottery-type feel. He liked them. They fit with who Elia was. She was delicate looking, but there was something solid beneath that veneer. Something that was more than just a pretty face. It made him glad, for some reason.

He accepted the plate with the small cakes Tersia had placed on it, waiting to see if they used forks to eat them or just their fingers.

Nelson seemed to sense his hesitation, because he glanced at him and then picked one up with his fingers and popped it into his mouth whole. Jake followed suit and a second later saw what the fuss was all about and why these were Elia's favorite dessert. Light and incredibly fluffy, it was like a cross between a donut and a sweet bread. And it melted in his mouth, making him want to repeat the experience.

Elia was watching him as she chewed her own cake, eyes closing for a second as she savored it before looking at him again and saying, "Good?"

"Very." And not only the cake. There was a sensual quality to the way she enjoyed the morsel that seemed to go beyond it as a simple food. And he'd enjoyed the sight a little too much, feeling a little like a voyeur who was watching something he shouldn't. Maybe because he was equating the food with sex. He could admit it, although he hoped to hell no one in this room guessed that little secret. To try to shake it from his thoughts, he popped another cake into his mouth. Except this time it was as if his perceptions had been altered, because he was letting it linger on his tongue just a little longer, trying to keep the sensation from ending.

Shit. He needed to get out of here.

His cell phone buzzed in his pocket, as if the universe had heard him. Taking it out to quickly glance at the screen in case it was an emergency, he saw it was indeed the hospital. "Sorry, I need to take this."

"Go ahead," Nelson said. "There's a balcony right through there, if you need some privacy."

"Thanks." As he walked toward the sliding glass doors, he was vaguely aware of someone else's phone ringing behind him. Glancing back, he saw Elia take her phone from her purse and glance down.

In the second that he went through the door that led to the balcony, he knew his escape wasn't going to be as easy as he'd hoped. He answered it and heard a panicked voice on the other end. "Jake. Can you come back to the hospital?"

"Sure." It was Sheryll calling. "What's up?"

"We've just had someone brought in who, according to a relative, had some kind of lye solution thrown on her by an ex-boyfriend. She's in bad shape."

"I'm on my way. Start lavaging the area immediately, but make sure you keep the water out of her eyes, in case there's any lye around them."

"Will do. I think one eye may already be compromised. Mary is trying to reach Elia to see if she can come, too. Do you know where she is? We're shorthanded and… Wait." She said something to someone in the background before coming back. "Never mind. We reached her. She's on her way in, too."

Elia evidently hadn't said anything about them eating together, so he decided to follow her lead. "Okay, I'll see you in about twenty minutes."

"Thanks." With that she hung up without saying goodbye. But Jake didn't need goodbyes. From what it sounded like, they needed a miracle. A big one.

Elia couldn't believe what she'd heard. She'd never dealt with a chemical burn that was on purpose before, although there were all kinds of ways that people hurt others. But to throw some type of caustic substance onto another human being... It was unfathomable.

Also unfathomable was the fact that she'd gone from laughing with Jake one minute to riding in his car as they each silently prepared for what they were about to find.

They burst through the emergency room doors, and as soon as the staff saw them they directed them to the burn unit.

"They've already transferred her since you guys have more of the needed equipment on hand to deal with serious burns," one of the residents said.

Jake kept moving, throwing back the words, "Nothing internal?"

"Not that we could assess. But the lye... It's caused quite a bit of damage."

Lye burns could be some of the worst, because you didn't immediately feel pain where the chemicals touched the skin. It was a case where the length of contact helped determine how much damage it caused to the skin and mucus membranes. It could literally dissolve tissue, turning it to jelly.

They caught the elevator just as the doors were opening. Jake didn't attempt to talk to Elia, but she couldn't blame him. He was probably running treatment options through his head, the same way she was. But even so, the silence wasn't an uncomfortable one and she didn't feel the need to try to break it.

Her mom and dad sometimes embarrassed her with their enthusiasm toward their guests when entertaining, but Jake hadn't seemed bothered. He'd seemed charmed by them, if anything.

As soon as the doors let them off on the floor, she glanced to the right where the empty nurses' station stood as a testament to the battle that was happening in one of the rooms, the one that people were going in and out of.

Jake nodded to one of the doctors who came out, an ophthalmic surgeon from the ground floor. "How's it looking?"

"She's almost certainly going to lose the right eye. The cornea is gone, and it's reached some of the deeper structures."

"Hell, how does something like this even happen?" the plastic surgeon asked.

"Breakups can bring out the 'mean' in some people. They feel like they have to hurt the other person back in some way. You know how *that* works."

Jake had a weird reaction to the words. He flinched, his head going back an inch or two. The other man didn't seem to notice, or if he did he didn't place much importance on it. "At least skin can be grafted, although her face is going to need some major work."

"Was it straight lye?"

"She evidently has a small business endeavor making homemade soap products. She was just adding lye to a wet solution when an ex-boyfriend came in and upended the folding table she was working on. She had eyeglasses on, but not safety goggles. He'd evidently made some threats, but nothing she'd taken seriously."

Elia started to edge past the two men so she could go in and help the team, when Jake put an end to the conversation. "Thanks. I'll get in there and see what I can do."

"Let me know. I'll be back in about a half hour. I have a procedure I've rescheduled three times already, and there's nothing more I can do for this patient right now."

With that, the young doctor strode toward the elevator they'd just exited.

They went through the door and found it was strewn with medical wrappers and containers. Two nurses stood next to a patient who was on a special table specifically made for lavaging large areas of the body. With raised sides that kept water and liquids contained, the head of the bed was slightly elevated so that everything flowed toward the base, where tubing was connected to a drain in the floor.

Sheryll came over to her. "Thank God, you're here. It's been just me and Mary, and she's not feeling well... Just went to the bathroom. Again."

As much as they were encouraged not to come in to work when ill, there were times when you just couldn't help it. At least when there was no fever, just a crappy sensation that you could sometimes work through. "Just tell me what you need."

"Patient's name is Dorothy White. We think we've lavaged long enough. But Timmons wants to get Jake's input."

Jeremy Timmons was a newer resident who was working under Jake's mentorship program. From what she understood, more and more cases were being shunted from a nearby hospital, which had just shut down their trauma department. It used to be that only the worst of the worst cases were sent to Westlake's burn unit for treatment after lifesaving triage—like this patient's lavaging—had already been done. But that meant some of them now had a longer ride in an ambulance to get to Westlake, which meant a longer time until they could get that treatment. She didn't know if that was the case for this particular patient, but when you were at home and unsure what to do for someone, it was hard. Westlake had hired Dr. Timmons right out of med school before another hospital could scoop him up.

"What needs to be done right now?"

"Let's see what Jake says. Can you stay here, so I can see to my other patients? It's been mass chaos up here for the last half hour."

"Go. I'm good."

Sheryll squeezed her arm. "Thanks."

With that the other nurse headed out of the room. Elia scrubbed up in a nearby sink and donned her PPE and then offered to help Jake as he did his. Two of the biggest dangers of large areas of tissue damage from burns were fluid loss and infections. Fluids could be replaced, but without the protective layer of the dermis, opportunistic bacteria were just waiting to move in. It was a continuous battle. And she'd seen one case where a patient with 90 percent burns was told he had little chance of survival. He was advised to say his goodbyes. It was one of the hardest cases she'd ever worked on. And true to what the doctors said, he died of sepsis two weeks after being burned, despite aggressive treatment with IV antibiotics.

Jake had instructed her to start treating the less serious burns with antibiotic cream, while he and Jeremy went over the patient with a fine-tooth comb and devised a treatment strategy that the two of them would carry out. Thankfully Dorothy, their patient, had received some sedation medication due to the extreme pain she'd been in.

"Are there any relatives here?"

"Her parents are out in the waiting room. They're pretty heartbroken, as you can imagine. We wanted to get her treated and in a room before we let them in. Dr. Perkins said to go ahead and tape gauze over the damaged eye before they see her."

Right now the patient's eyes were both closed, but the right lid was swollen and inflamed. She could only imagine the damage that lay below.

"The boyfriend is in custody, I hope?"

The last thing anyone wanted to deal with was an angry ex coming in and harming even more people. It was always a risk, but if you knew ahead of time, security could be increased.

"He was arrested at his home after fleeing the scene." Timmons looked up. "The guy had fixed himself a sandwich."

A wave of nausea washed over her. How could one human treat another like this and then go on as if it were nothing of importance?

She forced back the sensation and concentrated on what she was doing. This patient deserved her thoughts, not the man who'd done this to her.

Timmons came over to stand beside her. "How's it coming?"

"Just about finished with what I can see. Is there anything on her back?"

"Not much. Thankfully her clothing kept it from running down her back, although a little did get on her shoulder."

Looking at the right side of the patient's body, she could clearly see the swath of destruction where the caustic substance had either landed or had splashed as it hit. The damage ran from her eyebrow down to her right hip. Large blistered areas had already formed.

She and Jeremy discussed meds for a few more seconds before Jake came over, a slight frown on his face. Had he found something unexpected in his exam? She tilted her head. "Everything okay?"

"Yes, I just wanted to ask Jeremy if he'd go check on the parents and then make sure there's a room available so we can get her in and start debriding. Sooner rather than later."

Jeremy blinked at the man for a second before nodding. "Sure thing."

When he left the room, Elia said, "I could have done that."

"Her parents would expect one of her doctors to come out and talk to them."

Yes, she'd forgotten about that part of it, and

his explanation was perfectly plausible, but there'd been something in his face she hadn't quite been able to read. But it didn't matter. What did matter was getting Dorothy treated and stabilized. And as Jake had said, it needed to happen sooner rather than later.

CHAPTER NINE

FOUR HOURS LATER, Jake was finally satisfied with how the patient was doing. She was stable and all of her deep wounds had been debrided and covered with moist dressings. Dr. Perkins had seen to the right eye and declared it a complete loss.

Fortunately, or unfortunately, depending on how you looked at it, that was the worst of her facial wounds, although the lye had eaten down to the fat layer on one of her cheeks and was certainly going to need some grafting and plastic surgery.

He wasn't sure why he'd inserted himself between Jeremy and Elia earlier, other than the fact that he'd had an uneasy feeling about how close the man was to her and had reacted before he'd had a chance to think. Because really, Elia was right. She could have certainly gone to check on the scheduling at least.

But other than that, she hadn't seemed to

notice his gaffe. And he still wasn't sure what that had been about. What he'd said about the parents had certainly been true enough. It didn't matter. It was over and done, and Elia had done a great job in there. She hadn't had a single bobble or paused at anything he'd asked her to do during the procedures. It was as if they'd seamlessly worked together for years rather than just a few weeks. The hospital had certainly uncovered a treasure when they found her.

"Thanks for everything," he said. "I'm headed to my office to get some coffee. Can I interest you in some?"

She stretched, hands massaging the back of her neck for a second or two. "Yes. If I can sit down. I just want to get off my feet for a few minutes."

"My thoughts exactly. Right now even the thought of getting in my car is too much. These cases are hard. Damned hard."

As much as they'd tried to cover the worst of the burns to help ease the transition of her parents seeing her for the first time, they were certainly aware that the amount of bandaging was directly related to the amount of damage their daughter's skin had sustained. They were understandably upset by how she looked. And with the amount of painkillers she'd been given, Dorothy was only semiconscious. She was able to nod, but certainly not aware enough to carry on a whole conversation. And talking prognoses was another hard topic, but one that needed to be discussed.

"Yes they are. You handled the parents well, though."

"So I get a better rating than I did with Matt?" He could still vividly remember the first time he became aware of who she was. She'd been a fierce advocate of her patient and hadn't given a flying flip who Jake was or wasn't. He couldn't stop the slight smile that appeared.

She smiled back. "I'd give you a B."

"Not an A?" He was curious as to what her judging standards were. They reached his office and he unlocked the door, ushering her inside.

She seemed to think about the question for a minute. "My As are reserved for exemplary work. Which you may or may not have achieved. But I don't want you to get a big head."

That made him laugh. The horrors of what had happened to Dorothy weren't banished, but talking provided the means to transition back to their personal lives after the hard things they saw and did each and every day. Jake had seen excellent medical personnel burn out or their family lives destroyed from taking their work home with them one too many times. He'd learned to actively combat it.

She helped him fix the coffee as effortlessly as she'd worked beside him while treating their patient. He took a deep breath and allowed himself to relax. "Did you let your folks know you'd be late?"

"I did. My mom called halfway through the debridement procedure, so I stepped out and Sheryll covered for me."

He hadn't even noticed. But then again, his attention had been fixed on cutting open blisters and removing skin that was no longer viable. "Did you tell her not to wait up?"

She looked at him for a second before answering. "She already knows not to. In fact, she and my dad headed home right after she called since I have to work tomorrow."

"Hell, I'd forgotten that. And I drove us up here. Do you want me to just take you home?"

"No. Coffee sounds good. As long as you don't mind if I curl up on your couch to drink it. I need some time to decompress."

"Me, too."

She fixed her cup and then handed him the creamer. He glanced at the shelf where his mugs were. "Sorry I don't have espresso cups."

"It's okay. As long as your coffee is strong."

"It is." He followed her over to the sofa and sat next to her. And true to her word, she kicked off her Crocs and curled her legs up underneath her. It was cute and informal, and he found he liked it. A lot. "Not afraid the caffeine will keep you awake tonight?"

"It doesn't usually, and I'm so keyed up that it will actually help bring me down a little. And yes, I know that that doesn't make any sense."

"It does. Because I'm that way, too." He stretched his legs out in front of him and leaned back into the cushions like he normally did after he worked late. But he was always alone at those times. And he could pretty much count on himself to just fall asleep on the sofa. It was why he kept a clean change of clothes in his office. Fortunately his office had a bathroom connected to it. And the sofa actually pulled out into a bed. Although he couldn't remember ever using it. He normally just kicked his shoes off and pulled the large crocheted throw one of his patients had made him over himself and laid flat out on the couch.

They sat there for a few minutes before he said, "How's the leg?" As if worried about her reaction, he added, "Don't get upset. I just saw you massaging your neck and it made me wonder if it was bothering you. There's a blanket right beside you. You can use it if you're cold."

She frowned and glanced quickly down at her legs before tugging the fabric from her skirt to further cover her right ankle. Then she looked back up at him again as if trying to figure something out. She finally took a deep breath and blew it out. "No. I'm not cold, but thanks. And my leg is a little achy but not terribly. It's used to me being on it for long periods. But being able to bend them when I'm resting takes the strain off the scar contractures and makes it feel better. Are you sure it doesn't bother you? Some people don't like people putting their feet on their furniture."

"It doesn't bother me. I kind of like seeing you do it." The last sentence came out before he realized what he was saying.

But if she found it an odd thing for him to say, she didn't comment on it. Instead she tipped her head so that her cheek was lying against the back of the leather couch. "It's comfy. You should try it sometime."

"I'm not even sure my legs would bend into that position without breaking in half."

She smiled and, as always, it made something shift sideways in his gut. "Exaggerating at all?"

"Let's not try it and find out, is all I'm saying."

They sat there for a few seconds in silence. And he found he liked the quiet after the chaos in Dorothy's room. Then he said something he'd wanted to say ever since he'd thanked her outside of the treatment room. "You were a great asset in that room tonight. It was like you anticipated my every request. Not everyone has that ability."

"I think nurses overall do. But I also think because I didn't know much English when I came to the States, I had to learn to read body language to understand if what people were saying was something good, bad or of little importance."

That made sense. "Well, your English is excellent now, and I'm glad you haven't lost the ability to read people."

"I still have an accent that I can't quite shake. Rs are hard for me because they're pronounced so differently in Portuguese. 'Rural route' and 'squirrel' are superhard. I always want to put a *w* after the first *r* in squirrel. And rural route has three of those suckers." Her laughter tickled his insides and made his smile widen.

He could definitely hear what she was talking about when she said the word squirrel, and she overpronounced the second *r* in rural route, but he still found it attractive. And he really liked that she could admit that it was hard. Not everyone would.

"I hope you never lose that accent."

Her head was still resting against the sofa and she reached out to touch his arm. "That was an incredibly nice thing to say."

"Was it?"

She got very still. "It was. And I hope you never lose the ability to be as caring and nice as you are to your patients. As you are to me."

The world seemed to pause as he digested those words…as they found their way to a place inside that he hadn't opened to anyone in a long time.

He stared at her for a second and then leaned forward and kissed her. Only, unlike the last time, this one was on her mouth. And when he lingered a little longer, her mouth clung to his, her head coming off the back cushions to make better contact.

His hand slid behind her neck to support her when he changed the angle.

God, her mouth was sweet. Much sweeter than he'd imagined in the dark places of his mind, when he let himself think about it. Places he hadn't let surface entirely. Until now.

If she would have hesitated even the slightest bit, he would have stopped immediately and apologized, letting the chips fall where they may. But she evidently didn't mind. At all. Had she been thinking about him the way he'd been thinking about her when they'd been eating dinner with her folks?

He remembered her knee pressing against his and his reaction to it. If that call hadn't come in about an emergency, would the night have ended with a kiss the way it was now?

Too many what-ifs and not enough answers. But maybe that was a good thing. Because when she shifted her body so that she was facing him, she went onto her knees in order to do so, while his left arm went behind her back to pull her closer.

So much closer. Only it wasn't close enough for the impulses that were starting to gather around him, each one part of a long line of wants that were waiting for their chance to be heard. To be felt.

When he shifted Elia again, so that they were front to front, it seemed only natural that one of her knees should come across his thighs and land beside it on the couch. He saw her eyes go to the door before they came back to meet his.

"Do you want me to lock it?" The words seemed to gather in the center of the room as he waited for her reply. Her answer would say it all. Either she would shake her head no and get off his lap, probably beating a hasty retreat from his office. Or she would say yes and...

God, he hoped she said yes.

"No."

His hopes plummeted for a second before she added, "*I'll* do it."

Everything in him stood at attention as she did just that, climbing from his lap and going over to the door and turning the dead bolt above the handle.

He stood and went over to her, pulling her back against him, and then leaning over to kiss the nape of her neck. Her breath released in a whisper of sound that made his arms tighten around her midsection. All of a sudden he didn't care that she'd be able to feel his clear reaction to her nearness. That she would know exactly where he was hoping this would lead. And he was hoping.

Because if she changed her mind now, he was going to have a hard time explaining to his body why it couldn't have what it wanted. But he would. If she pulled away.

But she didn't. Instead, one of her arms came up to curl around the back of his neck and eased his head against her cheek. And when she turned her head…

His mouth covered hers, and this time there was no pretense. He let her know in no uncertain terms that he was okay with the locked door and everything that went along with it.

There would be no one to interrupt them. Sheryll had gone home and the staff that replaced her would assume he and Elia had followed suit and left the hospital, as well. If anyone needed them, they would call.

And he hoped to hell they didn't. At least not for a while. A very long while, if he got his wish.

When they parted, Elia turned toward him and he took a step back, using his index finger to signal for her to wait as he reached into his back pocket for his wallet, hoping he still had at least one of the packets he used to carry when he and Samantha were dating. He banished her name with a frown. He knew he had some at home, but to ask Elia to leave with him would spoil the mood and give him time to think about his actions, which he wasn't super anxious to do right now.

He flipped his wallet open and sure enough, tucked deep into one of the credit card holders was cellophane-wrapped protection. More than one. He pulled a single one out and then tossed his wallet onto his desk, not really caring where it landed.

Elia licked her lips, making him shudder with all he wanted to do with her. The pleasure he wanted to give her. The pleasure he wanted to take for himself.

He walked toward her with slow deliberation, twirling the packet between his fingers. His ex had started talking about children right about the time he'd started to have doubts about whether or not their futures were entwined together. Except she'd wanted those children to be carried by a surrogate, and that made him even more unsure, although he completely understood her reasons, since she was at the height of her career. But he remembered his mom talking about how excited she and his dad had been when they'd learned they were expecting him. How they'd gone through it all together and how it had drawn them even closer together.

And why was he thinking about all of this now?

He reached Elia and palmed both of her hips, loving the feel of her as he drew her a step closer and then two, until she was pressed tight to him, reigniting his senses and driving everything else away, like he'd hoped it would.

She surprised him by taking the packet from him and placing it on the desk beside him. But when he frowned, she shushed him, pressing her fingers to his lips. "When the time is right."

He swallowed. She was evidently all in but had some ideas of her own about how this was going to go down.

Her fingers trailed down either side of his face, starting at his temples, going over his cheeks, brushing over the stubble that wasn't quite a beard on his face, before reaching his neck. This time she softly raked her nails down his skin, the light pressure hitting all erogenous zones he didn't even know existed. He gave a low groan of approval and buried his fingers in the silky strands of hair beside her face, needing to touch her but not wanting her to stop what she was doing.

But she did stop. Long enough to reach for the bottom of his shirt and haul it up. He raised his arms and helped her take it the rest of the way off. Together they dropped it beside them. She cozied up to him, reaching up to place her lips on one of his shoulders in a warm, wet kiss that made him harden before nibbling her way down the front of his chest. And when she reached his nipple...

Heaven help him. Sensation rocketed out from where her teeth scraped over him and hit every nerve ending on his body. This time his groan was drawn somewhere from the pit of his gut, and he suddenly needed to touch more of her than was exposed. Needed something hot and intimate. She was still wearing the long gauzy skirt she'd had on for dinner, and he bunched it in his fist, moving his way down the fabric until he reached the hemline. Then he was at the skin of her left thigh and trailed up it, her mouth stopping its ministrations for a second before going back to what she was doing, her tongue licking over him like a cat.

A sexy siren of a cat who pushed all the right buttons and made him wish for more. So he gave it to himself, reaching the bottom of her panties. Without hesitation, he slid beneath them and found her wet and warm. So very warm. The urge to unzip and bury himself in that warmth came, and he waited until it passed before doing anything else. Because if he did what he wanted to, it was all going to be over much too soon. And he didn't want it to be over. He wanted to draw this out and experience every single thing he could.

He couldn't bury what he wanted to, but he could do other things. Like touch her. Slide into her with his fingers and use his mind to transfer the sensations to his own body as they happened. His thumb touched her lightly and she went stock-still. Then her hips inched toward him as if they couldn't control themselves.

Hell, yes. Just like that, baby.

His free arm went around the back of her butt, pulling her into his touch just as his fingers entered her. She shuddered, her head coming up to look at him, teeth digging into her bottom lip as he pushed deeper.

"Jakob." His whispered name came off her lips with a shaky tone that he loved. That contained that sexy little accent. That little stress happening on the last syllable, just like he thought it would.

He put his ear to her lips. "I love it when you say my name."

Her breath hissed out when his thumb became a little more insistent.

"I love it when you do that...just like that."

"Do you?"

"You know I do." She rocked against him. "But I want more. *Deus,* I want you. Not just your hand."

That did it. He was done fighting what he wanted to do. He withdrew and yanked her panties over her hips, going to his knees to let his hands trail the backs of her thighs as he carried them down. She tensed and reached for his arms, and he realized why when one of his palms crossed over a thick, uneven section of skin on her right leg and he realized it was her scar tissue.

"Shh...it's okay." His fingers stroked over the area with light wispy motions meant to soothe her.

He felt her muscles relax as she stepped out of her undergarment, only to stiffen up when he reached for the elastic waistline of her skirt. "No. Don't. Please."

His heart ached at the tone of her voice. Had someone said something about her leg? He remembered her wearing the long biker pants that covered everything up. And the skirt that came down to her ankles. He understood it, yet he wanted her to know she didn't need to worry. Not with him. But he needed to be careful. He wouldn't go against her wishes if she was set on staying covered up.

He looked up at her until he caught her eye. "Let me, Elia. Please."

Her teeth worried her lip again before she gave a hard nod, giving him permission. When he reached for the top of her skirt again, she didn't say anything, but her eyes closed tight, as if she couldn't bear to watch him take it off.

God, Elia. She had no idea how beautiful she was, with or without her scars.

He slowly peeled her skirt down over her hips, pushing it past her thigh, her knees...her ankles. And yes, her scars were deep and knotted and uneven, but they also told a story. One of overcoming a pain that went deep. Deeper than her physical injuries.

She lifted her feet one at a time and let him ease the fabric past them. He gingerly set the garment on top of his shirt. His palms massaged their way up both of her calves, giving no more attention to one than he did the other one. He went up her thighs, resisted doing what he really wanted to do. This was about acceptance and letting her know that she was perfect exactly the way she was. He planted a kiss on her right thigh where it joined her body.

"You are gorgeous, do you know that? So beautiful that you take my breath away." He climbed to his feet and used her hips to pull her back against him. "I want to do so much. So many things. But I don't think I'm going to be able to hold on long enough to do them all."

Her eyes reopened and the brown irises were warm, moist with what was maybe emotion. But he'd told the truth.

"You don't need to hold on." With that, she reached down and unzipped his trousers and unbuttoned them. He shoved them down and off his legs along with his briefs. Before he could reach for the condom, she beat him to it.

"Let me...please." She repeated the words he'd used earlier, her fingers brushing over his erection and making it jump as electricity seemed to sizzle across his skin. Only unlike him, she didn't wait for a response. Instead she tore open the packet and reached for him, palming him in her hand before her fingers closed over him, wrapping him in a tight band of warmth and stroking him.

"Hell... Elia. You need to stop." He reached

down and physically halted her movements before she drove him over the edge.

She gave a warm laugh and took a step back
until her backside was pressed against the
wood of his desk, avoiding the papers he had
stacked on one side. Then she put her hands on
either side of her thighs and hopped up until
she was sitting on top of it.

He'd had fantasies of that desk, but in it she'd
been leaning over it and he'd been behind her.
But this...this was even better.

She held the condom up in one hand and
motioned to him with the other. "Come here,
Jake."

He took a step forward, and she opened her
thighs to let him come between them. Then
she held him again, but not to torture him this
time. Instead she rolled the condom over him
until it reached the end of him. He wanted
to be buried in her the same way...until he
reached the very end.

He was so hard it hurt *not* to do anything.

But he didn't have to worry. She finished
what she was doing and then hooked her legs
around him, evidently no longer self-conscious
about her scars. Or maybe she was past the
point of being worried about anything.

So was he, because she hauled him against

her until there was nowhere to go but in. So he reached down and found her, his arms going around her ass and pressing home. The sensation was beyond anything he could describe, and he stood there wrapped tight in her heat for a few seconds before his mouth founds hers for a long searing kiss. His hands slid to her back, frowning slightly when they encountered fabric rather than bare skin. He leaned back so he could unbutton her blouse and let it fall open.

A pink bra met his gaze. It seemed so "Elia" that he let himself drink in the sight of those two perfect breasts cupped in lace. He pulled out slightly and thrust into her, watching them dance in time with his body.

Hell yeah. He loved the feel of her. The sight of her. He almost didn't want to take the bra off. Wanted to pump to completion as he watched them move. But like she'd said earlier, he needed more. More than just an animalistic act. He stripped off her shirt and then reached behind her for the hooks.

"It's in front."

Her fingers found the clasp and rotated it. Then the pink gave way and released her breasts. He wasn't sure why something that was made to feed babies created such an elemental reaction in him, but they did. He didn't need to rationalize it or explain it. He just loved the beauty of the female body. Each and every curve of it.

And then Elia did the unthinkable. She leaned back until she was lying across his desk, her body wide open to him.

Elia's eyes closed when his fingers curled around her hip bones and pulled her even more tightly against him.

Her nerve endings were singing, and between that and the way his body filled hers, stretching her, she felt things she'd never felt before, even though he wasn't her first lover.

But he was the first to make her feel like she was more than enough. The first one to actually ask her to let him uncover her legs to his eyes. The first one who made her want to say yes. And never once had he reached for that blanket on his sofa. It had taken a second, but she believed his offer had been sincere and had been precipitated out of concern for her comfort, not because of her scars.

He leaned over her, thrusting into her in a way that made her back slide over the cool smooth wood of his desk with each stroke. It was erotic and naughty in a way that was new to her. She'd always made love in beds. And once in a car. But never in a colleague's office.

She skipped over the boss part. He wasn't really. He didn't have the power to fire her. But he did have the power to light her on fire.

And he had. She was slowly being consumed by his heat. His eyes. The intensity of his body as he drew from her power, leaving her weak in the knees.

One of his hands left her hips and went up to cup her breast while still pumping inside of her. He didn't stroke it or squeeze it. And yet there was something so sensuous about it, as if he were feeling for something. Something that was only for him.

She couldn't stop the moan as her nipple went hard against his palm, as if trying to pleasure itself against his skin. She arched into his touch, her legs contracting against his butt, relishing the feel of the muscles in them as they tensed and released with each stroke of his body.

Keeping his one hand where it was, his other moved to where they were joined together and found that tiny little pleasure center and touched, pressing deep enough that her nerve endings were a ball of sudden need and heat. Jake leaned over her, his tempo changing.

Even though neither of his hands were moving in and of themselves, it was as if they were. As if they were stroking in time with his body, driving her higher and higher with each push and pull.

"Yes, Jake. *Deus. Quero te. Agora, quero...*"

He suddenly moved at a speed that caught up with her request and in a split second, he pushed her over the edge and into oblivion, where colors exploded behind her closed lids and her body contracted against his over and over again. Until his movements slowed. Still there was pleasure. Pleasure in the slow letdown that happened as his body came to a halt and rested against her. In the slow aftershocks that jarred her system and reminded her that she'd just been on top of a mountain.

One she needed to leave. In a minute. Maybe two.

Her hands fell to the sides and somehow managed to knock the stack of papers to her right off the side of his desk.

That had her plummeting back to earth. She sat up in a rush. "Sorry."

"It's okay. Don't worry about it." He glanced to the side, then gave a slight frown.

He pulled free more quickly than she anticipated, and her body gave a twinge of protest even as he was bending down to where the neat stack had become a scattered mess. The shiny cover of an entertainment paper came into view with the picture of a supermodel she'd seen on ads in various places. Bold headlines declared something about a renowned surgeon who'd abandoned her in France. Jake hurriedly scraped together other papers and piled them on top of what could only be a tabloid.

Why was it in his office? Maybe it had been left by a patient with whom he'd consulted in his office.

The way he'd just consulted with her?

The ugly thought floored her and she quickly suppressed it. She had not been unwilling or even hesitant. She'd beckoned him over with every intention of this ending exactly the way it had.

Well, maybe not with her knocking stuff over and kind of ruining her slow slide back to reality.

She hopped off the desk, but when she went to help him pick stuff up, he waved her away. "It's fine, really. There's nothing important."

And yet the way he was acting made her wonder.

Deus, she hoped things were not going to get weird.

Really? They were already weird. Really weird.

She bent down and grabbed her clothes, but when she made a move to yank them on in a hurry, he stopped her. Hauling her toward him and leaning close to kiss her, he murmured, "Everything okay between us?"

A second ago she would have said no, but the way he kissed her quieted those doubts. Her eyes skated over his desk, but the news article was nowhere in sight.

It wasn't important. He'd said it himself.

Her glance met his again and she let his warm smile lull her back to solid ground. He wasn't acting like things were awkward at all. But he also wasn't pressing her for anything more.

Which was a good thing. Right?

What had happened had to have been a simple release of adrenaline after their chaotic night. After fighting to help save someone's skin and possibly life, if the next few weeks were kind to her.

"Yes. Everything's good. But I really should get home and at least try to get a few hours of sleep. Unless you want to just crash on your couch. I can call a friend to come and get me."

She didn't say which friend, because she

couldn't really see herself calling anyone at two in the morning. But she could call a taxi or an Uber.

"No, I'll take you home. It's not a problem. Can I have five minutes? Unless you want to shower before we leave. There's probably room for two in there."

It was said with a wolfish charm that melted her heart. Okay, so it wasn't really like the proverbial "wham bam" scenario she'd just played in her head. Maybe he really would ease them back to more neutral territory. Like a one-night stand where acquaintances came together and then parted amicably, going back to whatever their previous relationship had been. People did it all the time.

Well, not her. Normally her exes disappeared into the mist never to be heard from again. Or she did. But there was almost never any contact between them again. She glanced at the undisturbed blanket on his sofa and a few of her muscles relaxed. This was a little more complicated because they worked together. But it didn't have to be.

And she could always put it off for a little while. Especially after the offer he'd just made.

She sent him a smile. "Well, as long as there's room for two..."

"If there's not, we'll make it work."

With one last glance at his desk, she followed him into the bathroom, her body already starting to hum with anticipation.

CHAPTER TEN

HE'D ENDED UP spending the night at Elia's apartment. In her bed. And they'd both definitely gotten less sleep than they'd anticipated.

But it had been worth it. And despite the horror he'd felt when that tabloid paper had fallen onto the ground in full view, she'd evidently not read the headline. Or at least she hadn't realized it was talking about him and Samantha.

But he'd left her apartment with a soft kiss and said he'd see her back at the hospital. And he had. And somehow, things had gone back to normal. For the last week they'd worked side by side, but neither mentioned the night they'd spent together.

Dorothy, their chemical burn victim, was doing better than anyone had hoped. She had lost her eye, but still had perfect vision in her left one and the ophthalmic surgeon had assured her that her eye socket was still in good shape and they could fit her with a prosthetic that no one would know was not her own eye, unless they looked closely. Her eyelid would have some scarring. And she would still need some grafts to cover her damaged cheek, but Jake was hopeful he could get it close enough to natural that she wouldn't feel self-conscious. He wanted to work hard to make that happen.

Because of Elia and how she'd balked at exposing her leg?

Maybe. But it was more than that. He wanted his patient to have the best possible outcome. He would say like any other patient, but he had to admit this one was special. Because of the night he'd spent with Elia?

Probably. But he was going to try his damnedest. For Dorothy. The same way he had for Matt, who'd done so well that he'd been released yesterday. The rest of his treatments and teeth implants could be done on an outpatient basis.

The world hadn't imploded after their night together. It had gone on spinning and patients had gone on recovering the way he'd hoped. And he and Elia had fallen back into an easy relationship with no talk about what had happened. It was the best possible scenario.

Although somewhere inside of him there was a little tick of dissatisfaction. And he had no idea what it was about. They really couldn't have an actual relationship. Like he'd told Sheryll, work romances normally turned messy. And for some reason he didn't want to lose the camaraderie he had with Eliana.

They were even planning to meet up at the bike festival tomorrow before the start. They hadn't made plans to necessarily ride side by side, but his bike club crew had decided to at least begin the race together, although they all knew they would eventually separate with the faster riders going out in front, just like they did with all their rides. Randy wouldn't be there for this one, since he was still healing from the injuries he'd sustained in the accident.

And man, that terrible event seemed like ages ago. So much had happened since then.

Originally he hadn't wanted Elia to continue riding with his club, but now he kind of hoped she did. The truth was, he liked being around her. Liked so much about her. He liked working with her and he loved how much she cared about their patients. In fact he loved...

Her.

He loved *her*.

Just then he saw her walking toward him and swallowed all of his thoughts in a big gulp that actually made a sound.

Don't make this awkward, Callin.

He'd probably been wrong. Yes. He had to have been mistaken. Then she smiled at him, and his system went haywire. He forced himself to smile back, but it was awkward.

Just like he was making everything all of a sudden. Awkward.

Even more awkward than when that tabloid paper had fallen on the ground right in front of her.

Well, he'd better figure out how to "unawkward" things right now, if he wanted things to stay the way they were.

And with all his heart he did. Because the idea of their relationship suddenly going sideways left a bad taste in his mouth. So it was up to him to figure out how to bury his feelings so deep that no one would ever find them. Even if he wanted them to.

The flare went off, signaling for the cyclists to start pedaling. There were over a thousand people gathered at the starting line. So many that it had taken Elia a while to locate Jake and his group. But they'd texted back and forth until she found them. The group stayed together for about a minute and a half before the leaders separated out. She was surprised Jake didn't go with them, but he hung back with her.

"Feel free to go on ahead. I don't expect you to stay here and babysit me."

His brows went up. "Do you *need* babysitting? Last I knew, you were all grown-up and able to decide things for yourself."

He probably hadn't meant anything by it, but her face turned hot as she remembered the last thing she'd decided for herself in the bedroom of her apartment. It involved her bathtub and acting out some of the fantasies she'd dreamed about the day of the accident in his tub. They were white-hot, and afterward he'd told her so. What she hadn't done that night was tell him where those ideas had come from.

"I am. But I know your club normally moves at a higher speed than my old one did."

He shrugged. "It's not really a race. It's a fundraiser. I'd rather sit back and enjoy myself."

Implying that he was enjoying himself by riding with her. This time the warmth that washed over her wasn't embarrassment, but pleasure. She was enjoying herself, too. And it had nothing to do with sex, but simply being in his company, something she'd missed in some of her other relationships.

Except this wasn't a relationship, unless they were doing things backward and letting the sex come before the friendship.

Would that really be so bad? Maybe not. But she had no idea if that was something Jake would want or if it was just her. Only she'd not even thought about it in those terms until this very second. And it would be better if she didn't until she could sit down by herself and think things through.

One thing she was thankful for, though, was the fact that the bike festival didn't take the same route as the bike club had on the day of that accident. She didn't know how she'd feel about passing that area and remembering the horror of it. She did wish Randy could ride this time, though. Jake said their club participated in the bike festival every year. The owner of the shop was here this time. And they all wore bracelets with Randy's name on them. She hadn't realized they were doing it until Jake had held one out and asked if she wanted to wear it. Of course she did. Made of leather and etched with his name, it was their way of saying he was missed and that they were riding in his honor.

This ride was only twenty kilometers, so it wouldn't take a huge amount of time, and there would be a cookout held at the park where the finish line was. Whoever wanted to stay could. Jake said it was fun, and there'd been a couple hundred cookies left that would be passed out on a first-come-first-served basis. It was kind of neat.

She glanced to the side just as he did, and they caught each other's eye and laughed. As if there was some kind of private joke. Of course there was. And it was very, very private. She'd told no one, not even her closest friends. Or her mom. This was for her and her alone. Well... her and Jake, since he obviously knew about it, too.

They chatted about Dorothy and Carly and Matt, and she asked what his hardest case was.

"Actually it was a case early on in my career. A Formula 1 driver's car caught on fire during a test run, and due to what they thought was a glitch, they had trouble getting the driver out. When they finally did, he'd been badly burned. He died hours after arriving at Westlake. It was a blow, since most of us knew who he was. Later on, it turned out his vehicle had been sabotaged by someone he'd fired from his pit crew."

"How terrible. Kind of like Dorothy's scorned

ex. I'll never understand how someone can hurt someone they supposedly love."

"People sometimes do things you'd never think them capable of doing." There was a hard set to his jaw as he said it.

"The most shocking thing is when there's no remorse afterward."

He glanced at her. "I agree."

They rode in silence for several more miles, but it seemed a little less relaxed than it was before. Because she'd brought up a memory that Jake would rather forget? She couldn't imagine how horrifying it would be to treat someone like the patient he'd had. Someone who was well known and whose case was probably reexamined countless times to see if anything had been missed. To see if something more could have been done. No doubt, Jake had already rehashed the timeline over and over.

She looked for a way to change the subject. "Does the bike festival ride the same route year after year?"

"They do. It's become a pretty big thing in the community. So much so that there will be people cheering us on as well as press at the finish line, so don't be surprised if one of them pulls you aside to do an impromptu interview."

"Yikes. With how sweaty I'm getting, that's the last thing I need."

He sent her a smile. "You look beautiful. No matter what."

Her face warmed. "I wasn't fishing for a compliment."

"And I wasn't dishing out fake praise."

"Okay, well, thank you."

He nodded toward the curve ahead as air horns sounded in the distance. "The finish line is just around that bend. Get ready to stop. It'll be pretty congested with folks getting off bikes and greeting family members."

It was then that she noticed more people standing on the sidelines waving flags with Westlake Memorial's logo on them. Wow, the ride had gone by really fast. She glanced at her watch, eyes widening. It had been two hours! It sure hadn't seemed that long. And she was kind of sad that it was over. At work, she and Jake saw each other in passing or while working on a case, but there wasn't much time for chitchat. Not like there was now.

She coasted as she neared the bend in the road, following Jake's lead, and as soon as they turned the corner, she saw he was right. Even though riders were being ushered off the course, people on bikes were standing around talking with pedestrians and other riders. Elia put on her brakes, and as soon as she slowed enough, she hopped off her bike. Jake did the same. It was mass chaos, and she wasn't sure where to go to get out of the path of those who were coming behind her.

"Come this way," he said. She followed him toward the edge of the pavement, where there was still a crush of people. But it was either that or risk being hit by another bicycle.

Suddenly there was someone with a microphone hurrying toward them. There was a photographer following close behind. Oh, no! She'd been serious about not wanting her picture taken looking like this.

"Dr. Callin!" the man called. "Dr. Callin! Excuse me, sir. How was the ride?"

Jake smiled. "It was great. Just like it is every year." He glanced back at her and made a move to go around the reporter only to have him step in front of him. "Just one more question. Any regrets since leaving Samantha Naughton behind in France a couple of years ago? I interviewed her a few months back, and she said she didn't understand what happened or why you left, but wished that you had stuck around. She said you were good together. She misses you."

A mental image of that tabloid article that

had been lying on the floor appeared in her brain. It had said that a doctor had abandoned the famous model in France...or something like that. Her head swiveled to look at Jake, who still had the same pleasant smile on his face, but a muscle was now ticking in his jaw.

Nossa Senhora, the article had been about Jake! He'd been the one to abandon Samantha. Why? How? And how could he not have mentioned that he'd been involved with the woman?

Why would he? She hadn't mentioned any of her exes to Jake. But she certainly hadn't left someone in a foreign country. Not that she'd traveled anywhere with any of her boyfriends. Except to maybe a local restaurant.

And Samantha Naughton? The woman was drop-dead gorgeous. And a great philanthropist, if the articles about her were to be believed. A huge wave of insecurity crashed over her. Jake had surely slept with the woman. Wouldn't you naturally make comparisons? Elia was not super experienced, and her embarrassment about her scars... Had she looked pitiful to him? He hadn't acted like it, but... He'd left his last girlfriend behind without saying a word about why, if the reporter was to be believed. But even the tabloids got some of the story right, didn't they? Otherwise they wouldn't sell so many copies.

Suddenly she was looking for a way to escape. She'd just headed toward an opening in the crowd when the reporter repeated the question again, this time asking if he was now dating "her" and pointing at Elia. Jake's smile disappeared and he gave the man an ugly glare before simply saying "no comment" in sharp tones. Then he sidestepped the cameraman and smoothly avoided the microphone and stalked away. He glanced back, as if trying to make sure that Elia was following him, but she wasn't. And she wouldn't. Her insides seemed to shrivel up into a tight ball. She couldn't get away fast enough from that look that had seemed to say, "Are you kidding me? *Her?*"

There was no way she could compete with someone like Jake's ex, nor did she want to. Even the thought made her close her eyes in horror.

Once past the crowd, she reached down to ease the strain on her right leg, giving her tight calf a quick squeeze. When she sat back up, Jake was there. "Sorry about that. Are you going to the cookout?"

Sorry about that? Was that all he had to say? He had to know she had a million questions going through her mind. "Um…no. Sorry." As she looked at him, her eyes started watering. *Deus.* There was no way she wanted him to see her break down, so she got on her bike and pedaled away from him—away from the event—as fast as she could without another word.

She knew they were expected to stay if they could, but if she tried, she didn't trust herself not to put on a huge show of waterworks. She just couldn't face Jake again, because somewhere in her heart, she had wanted him to tell that reporter that, yes, they were an item. Had maybe even believed that in her own heart or hoped it might someday be true. And yet that look on Jake's face… She just couldn't shake it. Just couldn't fathom why he'd wanted to sleep with her in the first place. Or why she ever could have thought they might one day be together. How big of a fool was she?

He had walked away from someone like Samantha Naughton. How much easier would it be to walk away from naive Elia Pessoa, who believed the best of people until proven wrong?

Well, it looked like she'd just been proven wrong. Big time. And she had only herself to blame for some baseless romantic notions she'd allowed herself to harbor. Thank heaven someone had burst her bubble before she'd made a complete fool of herself. Time to find a dark corner in her house and sit and lick her wounds for a while. Thank God she didn't work tomorrow because she was not ready to face the man again. Not today. Not tomorrow. But she'd better figure things out before Monday. Because he was going to be at the hospital. And so was she.

After a week of trying to corner her long enough to talk to her, Jake realized Elia was actively avoiding him. Ever since the bike festival when he tried to talk to her at the end. Because the reporter had asked him if they were a couple?

He could only take that to mean that she didn't want them to be a couple. Ever. Especially since she couldn't even stand being in the same room with him, even at the hospital.

Just when he'd started thinking he might have it in him to give love another go. Would she send her people over to tell him no way, no how? Hell, he didn't even know who Elia's "people" were.

Yesterday he had gone to the hospital administrator and told him he needed a break. That he trusted Jeremy Timmons to handle his cases while he was gone. The only good thing was that Jake had not seen anything in the tabloids about the reporter's comments. He guessed the hospital had been right in their recommendation about not engaging when asked a stupid question. And how about Samantha saying what she had. Or had the reporter simply been fishing for a story? Who the hell knew? Or even cared?

He had a little place in Ensenada, Mexico, right on the Baja California peninsula that had been left to him by his father. It was a place filled with wonderful memories of childhood vacations. Maybe it would serve as a good place to clear his head. To reset his future. He'd already booked his flight for tomorrow, and the plan was to stay for two weeks, although he hadn't given the administrator a fixed date. He hoped to hell that was long enough. And honestly, it didn't matter. Because long enough or not, he was going to have to figure out how to go back to working with Elia. Or he was going to have to quit his job and go somewhere else.

Jake was gone? He wasn't at work today and no one seemed to know where he was or when he'd be back.

Elia had come into work after making a decision. She was going to have to have it out with him. Her work was suffering, and she knew Sheryll had given her several inscrutable looks, like when she'd caught her ducking around a corner in the middle of rounds, when she'd spied Jake heading out onto the floor. Sheryll hadn't come right out and asked her, but she knew the questions were coming if she kept it up.

She really didn't want to get fired. Jake didn't have to tell her anything about what had happened with Samantha, but she needed to tell him that she wasn't looking for a relationship of any kind with him. Physical or romantic. Because it turned out—for her, anyway—that she didn't have it in her to be a friend-with-benefits kind of girl. If the physical didn't at least have the possibility of romance attached to it, it wasn't sustainable on her end. And she didn't want to always wonder if comparisons were being made. So it was better just to come out and make things as plain as she could make them.

Except he wasn't here. And no one could give her a straight answer as to how long he'd be away. Dr. Timmons was taking over his cases. Which meant whatever was wrong had to be kind of serious, didn't it?

An ugly thought slithered into her head and

coiled there, waiting to strike. What if the reporter had been right about Samantha missing him? What if Jake had called her and even now they were rekindling their romance?

Her insides squelched, her lunch sloshing around as if seeking an exit. The way she had looked for an exit at the bike festival? She'd heard they'd raised a record number of funds that would go directly to the burn unit this year. A picture of one of her mom's cookies had even made the local papers. Sheryll showed her the picture that morning. As soon as she got home that afternoon, she called her mom, who answered on the first ring.

"Hi, sweetheart. How are you?"

Elia mentally switched over to Portuguese, knowing her mom preferred it. "Doing okay…" Her voice faded away and the next thing she knew she was crying, sobbing into the phone like her heart was breaking. Because it was.

"Elia! Elia! *O que é?*"

Her mom asked over and over what was wrong, but Elia just couldn't get the words out. She tried, but nothing came out except these wrenching cries of pain.

"Is it that Jake?"

She cried even harder.

"Elia, *filha*, I am on my way."

"No…" She still couldn't talk. And she realized she wanted her to come, needed her mom to hold her and tell her she hadn't been a complete fool, whether it was true or not.

As soon as her mom hung up, a text pinged on her phone.

Do I need to call an ambulance for you?

She scrubbed the tears from her eyes with balled fists.

No. Sorry. Just dealing with some stuff.

Stuff. Jake stuff?

Elia hesitated for a long time with her answer. She didn't want her mom to have to drive three hours just to hear some nonsense about Jake. But her fingers seemed to type of their own volition.

Yes, it's about Jake. And I sure could use some advice.

Good. Because I'm already in the car with a packed bag.

Three hours later, her mom came through the door and Elia fell into her arms. She was past the point of crying, having gotten most of that out hours ago. Now she was just numb.

They sat on the couch, and Elia spilled the beans about all of it. How they had worked on a case and had gotten caught up in the emotions of it all and spent the night together. About how they'd ridden in the bike festival together and the part about the reporter and his questions.

"Did he actually respond to the question about whether you were his current girl-friend?"

"No. But the look on his face…"

Her mom tilted her head. "What about it?"

"It was filled with such…disgust." The tears she thought were long gone surfaced all over again.

Her mom scooted over and put her arm around her. "Look at me."

Pulling in a deep breath, she turned to face her.

"*Filha*, I am only going to say this one time. No one who ever looks at you could be filled with disgust. A man doesn't sleep with some-one who makes him feel that way. His…er… *coisa*, shall we say, would not stand at atten-tion for someone who disgusts him."

"*Mamãe!*"

"Well, it is true. Did you ask the man why he looked the way he did?"

"No. I just couldn't bring myself to."

Her mom sighed. "Could it not be that the disgust was aimed at the reporter? Not at whether or not the statement was true?"

"I don't know. I never stopped to think about that."

"Go talk to him. Ask him. If he doesn't care about you, that will be his chance to say so, but if he does..."

Oh, Lord. Not only had she not talked to him when she'd had the chance, she'd rebuffed every attempt that he'd made to talk to her. She assumed he was going to try to let her down easy. But she realized her mind had concocted such a crazy jumble of possibilities that it was very likely none of them were true.

And what about Samantha?

Well, she would never know unless she asked him.

"He tried to talk to me, I think, but I assumed the worst and avoided him, and now..."

"And now what?"

"He left the hospital, and I'm not exactly sure where he went or how long he'll be gone. Maybe he'll never be back."

Her mom squeezed her tight for a second.

"Could it be that Jake is struggling with some of the same things you are?"

"But what if he's not? What if he just doesn't want to see me?"

"But what if he does and is afraid, just like you are? What if after trying to talk to you he assumed the worst, that you didn't want him?"

Why did her mom have to make her see things with such glaring clarity? "And if it's him who doesn't want me?"

"Then you'll know. Life is not without risks, Elia. The doctors told us you might not keep your leg, that the vascular system was badly damaged and it could die. They wanted to amputate. I kept saying to wait...wait...wait, that I would know when the time was right. It never was. That you can walk is a miracle in itself."

"I didn't know that about my leg."

She shrugged. "Just like with the doctors, I felt something was telling me to wait to tell you. That I would know when the time was right. That time is now. Don't cut out part of your heart without at least giving it a chance to heal...without giving it a chance to know the truth."

"But he's gone. I'll need to wait until he—"

"No. You need to decide what it is you want out of life. If you want Jake, you shouldn't wait for him to come to you. He tried. It is now time for you to go to him."

"But how? I don't even know where he is."

"Ask. Ask those who might know. And keep asking until someone can give you the answer you are looking for."

Jake was packing his bags. This was the most ridiculous idea he'd ever had. Had he really thought the answers would magically appear the second he stepped over the threshold of the little two-bedroom bungalow?

They hadn't. And he found he missed Elia like he'd never missed anyone in his life. It was crazy. And terrible.

She wouldn't talk to him, but somehow he had to know one way or the other without looking like some kind of crazed stalker. He'd thought about texting her, but this needed to be a face-to-face conversation. Maybe once that happened, no matter which way that discussion went, he'd finally have a peace about the situation.

Yes. In his soul of souls he somehow knew that was the right way to go. He couldn't text her with the question, but he could text a request for a meeting. He could say they needed to clear the air about a few things. And if she still said no? Then maybe he'd have his answer. He'd never actually gotten that far. She always ducked out the second he appeared. Maybe she was horrified that he'd supposedly abandoned Samantha. Then he could explain he hadn't.

He sucked down a breath and let it hiss back out. That was it. He was going to send that text and then he was going to catch his flight.

He looked up her phone number. When he went to compose the message, he found their back-and-forth texts about where the bike crew was. They were witty little comebacks with a couple of barely hidden innuendos. How had that gone from warm and fun to her wanting to be as far away from him as she could possibly get?

It was after that reporter's questions. He tried to recall exactly what had been said. There'd been the questions about Samantha. Those had surprised him, but they hadn't been totally out of the blue. What had embarrassed him, though, was how it made him sound. He couldn't get out of there fast enough. And then the reporter had asked about Elia and their relationship. And Jake's reply? "No comment."

He shut his eyes. "Oh, Callin, you really are a fool." No wonder she didn't want to talk to him. He could imagine how it might have sounded to her.

He composed his text carefully.

Hey, beautiful...

Nope. He erased the last word. Too forward.

Hey, Elia... Is there a time we could talk? I would like to explain something I said to the reporter that I think you might have misunderstood. I'd like to clear the air and tell you what I would have liked to have told him.

Yes. That was okay. If he was right about why she was upset, then hopefully she would want to hear the truth. Holding his breath, he pressed Send.

Then, picking his bag up, he opened the door only to hear his phone ping from his pocket. Frowning, he fished it out again and looked at the screen.

Can you give me your address? I'm hopelessly lost.

What in the...?

He looked at the top of the screen and saw the series of earlier texts. Yep, it was from Elia.

I'm not in the States at the moment, so I'm not home.

Wait, why was she trying to find him, anyway?

I know. I'm in Ensenada. But, strangely enough, the taxi driver doesn't know who you are or how to find you. I thought everyone knew who the great Jakob Callin was.

He mentally heard her saying the words in that accent of hers, right down to his name. He swallowed, loving so much about the woman.

It finally sank in. She was in Ensenada! She was here in town. But how?

Where are you, exactly?

Her text came through almost immediately.

Some grocery store called Mi Corazon.

Stay there.

No, just give me your address. I'm in the taxi now.

He typed the address and waited for her reply.

Nothing came through.

Two minutes passed before he texted her again.

Elia?

Give me a minute...

What the hell was going on? That grocery store was just around the corner from his house. Just as he got ready to text her again, there was a knock at the door.

When he opened it, there stood Elia. Just beyond her was a taxi.

"Does he need to be paid?"

"No, I just... I just wanted him to wait in case it wasn't really you."

The tremor in her voice cut him to the quick, and he folded her into his arms, waving away the taxi and closing the door. Easing her away from him, he looked into her face. "I won't ask how in the hell you found me. Instead, I'll simply ask you why you're here."

"I'm here because my mom suggested I come."

"Your mom." He was lost. What did Tersia have to do with any of this? "She told you to come to Mexico?"

"No. She told me to come find you before it

was too late. She told me about risks and that I'd almost lost my leg as a child, but she'd insisted they wait... Oh, too many things to explain." She took a deep breath. "I love you. And in my heart, I needed to know if you were here with Samantha."

"Samantha? I haven't talked to her since we broke up. Nor do I plan to. She and I were a mistake. One that I don't plan on making again."

She seemed to straighten slightly. "You said I misunderstood something about your conversation with that reporter. What was it?"

He drew her inside and sat with her on the long leather sofa in the main room. "When Samantha and I broke up, she told a tabloid reporter that I had 'abandoned her' in France. It wasn't true. I wasn't even there at the time, but it caused some problems for me at the hospital. Their suggestion if a reporter ever brought it up again was to say 'no comment' and leave it at that." His mind rewound to a previous comment she'd made. "Wait. What did you say a minute ago?"

"About Samantha?"

"No. Right before that."

She smiled. "Oh, that. I love you."

He sat there, stunned. "Why didn't you tell me this when I tried to talk to you?"

"Because…" She bit her lip before continuing. "When the reporter asked about me, you had this terrible look on your face. Like you were stunned that he would even ask that."

"I was stunned. And very, very angry." He tried to find the words. "I'd realized something right before the race. That I wanted to continue seeing you. And not just because of the sex. Because of you. But I wanted to move slowly and see if you were even interested in me. And then that guy comes right out and asks if you were my new girlfriend. I just lost it. I really wanted to do some damage to him, and so I walked away before I acted on that impulse. I think that's what you maybe misunderstood."

She nodded. "The look on your face… It was as if the very thought disgusted you. My mom assured me that if that were the case, your— she used the word equipment, for lack of a better translation—wouldn't work properly."

Jake laughed. It was the first time he'd done that in a while. "Can you tell your mom that I love her? And you?"

"Really?"

"Yes." He bent down to kiss her. "And your

mom is right. My 'equipment' is very...*very*... active whenever you're around."

"But Samantha is just so beautiful."

"Do you seriously think you're not?"

She stumbled, as if not sure what to say.

"Elia, there is so much about you that fascinates me. I can't get my fill of looking at you. Of touching you...like this." He trailed the back of his hand from her cheek to the spot just behind her ear.

"I can't think when you do that."

He smiled. "Do you need to think?"

"Just for a few minutes. Just long enough to know for sure. You really love me?"

"Yes. I really do." He turned her so that he could look into her beautiful eyes. "Do you love me?"

"Yes."

His lips touched the side of her temple. "Anything else?" They trailed across her cheek on a slow journey back to her mouth and paused there, waiting for anything else that she needed him to clarify. "Elia?"

"Hmm...just one more thing."

He kissed her mouth with slow brushing strokes that only made him want more. "What is it?"

"Are you coming back to Dallas?"

"Yes, my bags are packed and I was on my way out the door when your text came through. My flight is in an hour. We can just make it, unless…"

"Unless what?"

"Unless you'd like to spend a few days here instead."

Her eyes widened. "Seriously?"

"Yup."

When her smile came, it was like the sun itself had stepped into the room. "Yes. Let's stay."

His arms wrapped around her, gripping her tightly. "This place has two bedrooms if you'd rather—"

"Yes." When his heart dropped, she added with a smile, "We'll spend one night in one of them and the next… Well, let's see if we even make it out of that first one before it's time to leave."

His equipment rose, right on cue. "Is that a challenge, Elia?"

"Only if you want it to be, *querida*. Only if you want it to be."

And then she was kissing him in a way that said all other questions could wait until they were back in the States. Until then, he would show her exactly how much he loved her. How much he wanted her. And he'd keep on showing her all the days of his life.

EPILOGUE

THE BIKE SHOP was full of bicycles, as would be expected. What wasn't quite so expected were the twirls of white streamers that covered the ceiling. Or the satin kneeling bench that sat at the front of the shop.

But Elia had never seen a more beautiful sight in all her life. The owner of the bike shop, where she and Jake had ridden for the last six months, knew someone who knew someone who was a licensed minister. He'd been willing to come and marry them. In the bike shop. And she couldn't think of a more perfect setting, since it was one of the things that had brought them together.

Randy was all healed up from that terrible accident and stood beside Jake as his best man. And Sheryll was there for Elia, who had chosen a white silk gown that hugged all her curves. It was simple, but evidently met with

Jake's approval—he hadn't taken his eyes off her since she'd emerged from the door of the shop's office a minute or two ago.

He came to her and took her hands, leaning down to give her a soft kiss on the mouth that drew some noise from the dozen or so friends and family that were seated in folding chairs behind them. She smiled at her mom and dad and Tomás, who sat in front, along with Jake's mom. There were so many other people in attendance who had become important in her life since she'd come to work at Westlake Memorial.

Gracie and Matt had made it to their prom. Jake had a picture of the couple taped to his refrigerator. Gracie had worn a purple gown for the event, and Matt had a tie that matched her dress exactly. And she'd looked so proud as she huddled close to Matt, her hand pressed tight against his abdomen, as if warning other girls away. And like Jake, Gracie hadn't balked even for a second at embracing who Matt still was. Yes, there were some scars, but if anything, their young relationship had blossomed as they'd gone through therapy and his treatments together. Gracie waved at her, and Elia's smile widened as she waved back.

Carly and her parents weren't in attendance, but they'd kept in touch after leaving the hospital and had sent news that their daughter had just started preschool and was doing wonderfully. It was another photo on their refrigerator. They hadn't been able to be there due to a scheduling conflict, but someone who *was* there was Dorothy. Elia's heart had ached so much for the young woman, but Dorothy had shared that rather than letting her injuries defeat her, they'd given her a sense of control that she hadn't felt in a long time. *She* would decide her own next steps. Her cheek was red from a second skin graft surgery, but she'd done remarkably well through it all.

Elia wouldn't wish what had happened in her childhood on anyone, but that terrible occurrence had been the catalyst that had set her life on a course that ended right where it was now: getting ready to marry the love of her life. Correction. That wasn't an ending. It was a beginning. The perfect one with the perfect person.

Someone who loved every inch of her and wasn't afraid to show it. Someone who shared things with her that no one else knew. That let her take some of his pain when a case rocked him to his core. And he did the same for her.

When one was weak or sad or afraid, the other was strong and supportive. Everything a partner should be. And Elia wouldn't have it any other way.

As they turned to face the minister, she glanced up at her husband-to-be and whispered, "I love you."

He swept a stray tendril from her cheek. "Love you, too."

With that, the reverend opened the service. "Dearly beloved, we are gathered here today..."

She threaded her arm through Jake's and pressed close to his side, needing nothing else in these next moments than the joy of being here with him. Of being with those they both loved. And agreeing together that they would take the love that bound them to each other and do great things with it. Not just for each other, but for those they came in contact with each and every day.

And Elia could think of no better person to do that with than Jake. Her strong, handsome, kind and so very sexy man. The one she intended to spend her whole life with. The one she wanted to live with, love with and have children with. Including the one they were expecting in the next six months.

Life was perfect. *He* was perfect. And she was going to make sure she told him so each and every day. Starting today.

* * * * *

If you enjoyed this story, check out these other great reads from Tina Beckett

A Daddy for the Midwife's Twins?
Resisting the Brooding Heart Surgeon
The Surgeon She Could Never Forget
The Nurse's One-Night Baby

All available now!